CORDELIA'S SPIRIT

David Stanley

Book 3 in the series:

Book 1: Cordelia's Song
Book 2: Cordelia's Heart
All books are available from
www.morrispublishingaustralia.com

Morris Publishing Australia

CORDELIA'S SPIRIT

ISBN: 978-1-7635669-3-4

Morris Publishing Australia

www.morrispublishingaustralia.com

DEDICATION

iii

To all creatures great and small
(it can be a hard world for the little things)

NOTES

This is the third book in the Cordelia saga.

Cordelia's Spirit begins immediately after Cordelia returns to the valley and after the new building development in the eucalyptus forest has been halted. In essence, it picks up from where *Cordelia's Heart* finished and completes the story of *Cordelia's Song*. Like the first part of the story, it is completely fictional, although in my mind, the valley, and the adventures of Cordelia and her friends occur in the Australian state of New South Wales.

All characters, locations and names used in the book are fictional and bear no intentional resemblance to any person (or bird) known to the author, living or dead. The fictional names for the animals and other specific items in the book are all invented by the author, and if they have any resemblance to First Nations words or indeed words from any other culture, they are purely coincidental. The world of the 'mytre' (magpie) set before the reader is the result of the authors imagination alone. The valley, and the other locations are completely fictional although they were inspired by visiting a conglomerate of similar places across rural New South Wales.

There's nothin' you can do that can't be done

Nothin' you can sing that can't be sung

Nothin' you can say, but you can learn how to play the game

It's easy

Nothin' you can make that can't be made

No one you can save that can't be saved

Nothin' you can do, but you can learn how to be you in time

It's easy

All you need is love

All you need is love

The Beatles – 'All you Need is Love' (1967)

Contents

GLOSSARY

A list of Magpie (Mytre) words used in this book.

MAGPIE (MYTRE) WORDS)

GODS:

Egnaro	= The God of the Moon, the night the bringer of cold and darkness
Elppa	= The God of the Sun, the day the bringer of light and warmth
Korzela	= The God of Wind
Xervinu	= The God of Rain

TIMES OF DAY

Ksud	= Dusk
Nwad	= Dawn
Nwod	= High sun or noon

OTHER MAGPIE (MYTRE) WORDS USED IN THE STORY

Elpitlum	= Community/clan meeting or large gathering of birds.
Keere	= Monster or evil thing (anything that kills mytre)
Mytre	= Magpie
Norzela	= Humans
Norzela Nest	= Human house/home
Norzela Park	= Human golf course
Picture Window-Box	= TV

PREFACE

The Valley

Cordelia's story takes place in the valley. Cordelia's home and the sky she learnt to fly in. It was here that her father died and here that she found her voice and capacity to stand up for what she believed. It was also in the valley that she found love in the form of Barry, a mytre from another clan and in the valley where she brought all the valley clans together to fight off the lizard invasion. Cordelia returns to the valley from the battle with Silas on the escarpment, not aware that she has been followed back into the lower valley by a cat.

But Cordelia's powers of perception remain strong and even as she and Barry and the other mytre settled back into life in the valley, Cordelia becomes increasingly aware that all is not as it should be, and that she will need to be strong and fight for her home and sky.

High above the destruction of valley a scout patrol made up on Karnny and Waytsill flew close together in formation with one bird slightly in front of the other. Each scanned the sky around them and the trees below. They saw Cordelia and Barry hop flap through the foliage on the middle valley almost back near the dam that marked the beginning of their territory. They each called out to Cordelia from high above signalling that all was well.

They flew off toward the foot of the escarpment to continue their search and watch over their fellow clan members and their homes. Once they'd passed into the distance Cordelia quickened her hop steps despite the pain in her injured shoulder. She was glad to be almost home where she could rest and consider her feelings of disquiet.

PART 1

A CAT COMES TO THE VALLEY

1
A BOWER

Blown too much of me time buying dinner and wine
And me money on flowers and lollies
Only to find that what's on me mind
Isn't on hers and she's sorry
So I've made up some lines that save wastin' time
And keep me from blowin' me brass
I'm ever so cool I just prop on the stool
Right next to hers and I ask:

Kevin Bloody Wilson – 'The Courting Song' (1993)

THE SATIN BOWERBIRD stood back and admired his work. His blue-black plumage had taken seven years to grow to maturity and his vibrant violet eyes looked upon his creation, his bower, with satisfaction. His name was Phil, and he'd been a resident of the upper valley all his life. He'd begun his bower when he'd been young, and it had taken almost his whole life to perfect and construct the magnificent structure he'd stepped back to observe.

The bower site was high up the valley almost at the foot of the escarpment wall and it sat in a small clearing between two stubby wattle trees. Ferns, Davalliancear, Adiantaceae, and Marattiaceae or King fern, and a wide variety of bottlebrush, Callistemon glaucus or swamp bottlebrush, Callistemon pearsonii or blackdown bottlebrush and even Callistemon pinifolius or pine-leaved bottle brush grew all around the small gully it was in. The ferns and other shrubs surrounded the small clearing, making the bower appear to standout, like a norzela stage or a rotunda in a tree filled park.

The bower was an avenue-type structure made from sticks and twigs so that it resembled a hollow tunnel with the sticks rising like a neatly woven basket, with sides touching but not intertwining at the top. It was at least twice Phil's height and wide enough for the satin bowerbird to pass through the tunnel from front to back or vice-versa. The tunnel's front was strewn with stones gathered from the escarpment's base and mixed throughout the stone garden were dozens of blue objects, not usually seen in the shady areas of the upper valley.

Bottle tops, lids of pens, clothes pegs, small plastic toys, blue plastic tags from bags of bread, blue fragments of broken glass, and the ring pulls from cans of drink were scattered around. The rear garden of the bower was not as elaborately decorated and while there were some stones strewn about the ground, the main attraction apart from the cathedral like wooden spires of the bower, were the collection of blue oddments spread around.

Phil also used an optical illusion to attract his potential mate by placing the larger blue ornaments further from the bowers entrance and the smaller ones closer to it, creating the illusion of depth and increasing the beauty and apparent size of the bower. It acted like a slope leading the eyes of the potential female to the entrance of the bower, where Phil would perform his elaborate dance and sing his mimicked songs.

Phil's bower was also covered with small blue flowers and berries taken from nearby trees and shrubs. Phil had found a small blue pincushion plant (Brunonia Australis) near his bower and used the small semi-sphere like, corn-blue flowers to decorate his bower. As well, there were a few dark blue flowers from the royal bluebell plant (Wahlenbergia Gloriosa) spread amongst the twigs and stems of the bower. These added a splash of deep blue colour to the stems and twigs of the bower's structure and made the whole construction pop with a blue glow.

It was especially dazzling as the noon rays of Elppa penetrated the low canopy of trees and glistened on the ring pulls and shiny blue objects spread around the bower. Phil had failed to attract a mate in previous years, but this year, this year... he'd done all he could and as he waited for a potential mate to appear, he was suddenly aware of a set of iridescent eyes, violet blue eyes, peering at him from under a nearby fern.

The female satin bowerbird had drab brown-green coloured plumage and a pale underbelly. She'd visited two other bowers that day and was seemingly impressed with Phil's completed bower. They had met before. She was called Iris. Phil hoped she would return and be impressed with his construction. *This bower looks magnificent,* Iris thought, as she inspected his home.

Phil broke into song the moment he was aware that she was present. Phil was a superb vocal mimic. His first call was that of a carolling magpie-lark singing *peewee, peewee*, over and over as if a magpie-lark had suddenly appeared in the bower. As he sang, the watching female moved a little closer toward the bower, intrigued.

Phil continued to sing but switched to the *quadle-oodle-ardle-wadle-doodle* song of the Australian mytre. He knew this was a beautiful song and he'd practiced almost daily for a long time to perfect his enticing carolling. As he did, he began to dance in and out of the front entrance to the bower, bowing low and standing tall as he sang. Iris, his potential mate, approached a little further, trying to see the detail of the objects collected and to admire his building skills.

Phil then began his most intricate song, imitating the *tsit, tsit,* and *chit, chit* of the superb fairy wren, adding short notes and accelerating them with rippling trills. As he did, he took hold of some of the larger blue objects and carried them into the bower, as if inviting her to inspect his treasures within the walls of his construction. She seemed to be totally engrossed in his display. Finally, after years of preparation, hard work, and practice, he felt this courtship dance would lead to him finding a suitable mate.

But Phil didn't know his dance and songs were being watched by another set of eyes. This second pair of eyes, although attracted by his songs were not at all interested in his suitability as a mate, or talent as a mimic singer or in his bower building skills.

All the ginger cat saw was lunch. Phil, returned to mimicking the magpie-lark's *peewee, peewee* song, as he sensed the female bowerbird was finally ready to join him in his bower. Suddenly, she took to wing and flew with a shriek of alarm. Phil was gobsmacked. *How rude*, he thought as he watched her scurry off through the ferns and low tree branches at haste, away from his beautifully built structure.

In a moment she'd gone, and he felt suddenly despondent. Years of effort, building the bower, waiting patiently for his plumage to turn to the stunning blue-black tones of a mature satin bowerbird. Now she'd been spooked or seen something that she'd not liked in his display and gone. *Damn it*, he thought. *I was sure she liked me.*

Then she struck.

The ginger cat had been watching the courtship display and waited, hoping to catch both birds, but she'd been seen by the female as she made her final tentative steps toward the bower. She'd seen the cat crouched behind the rear entrance of the bower and it was this that terrorised the female bowerbird into flight. Phil was at first focused only on his dance and song, and once she'd flown, he was overcome with feelings of disappointment, loss, and frustration… he still hadn't seen the cat's approach. He turned to pick up the light blue piece of glass he'd moved into the bower and was about to replace it when the cat attacked.

She sprang forward through the bower using its sides to her advantage. Phil found he couldn't turn to flee or rise into the air.

Trapped in the bower the ginger cat grasped him by the throat and held the flapping bird tightly. Phil tried with all his might to retreat, to call out and to kick out at the terror before him but he was held too tightly and although he flapped mightily, he couldn't break free.

Phil was not a small bird but there was little he could do as the lean, ginger hunter pinned him down and choked off his airway. *At least 'she' escaped*, Phil thought, thinking of his potential mate at the end. It was his last thought and as the feral ginger cat choked Phil by gripping his throat in her jaws.

The last noise he made as a whisper with his last breath, was her name… "Iris." Her name lingered in the air within the bower that had become his doom. He thought, A*t least her name is here with me at the end*.

The feral cat dragged Phil's body through the bower, taking no care as she knocked and twisted the stems and twigs out of place and disturbed the neatly arranged blue trinkets, he'd spent a lifetime collecting.

No longer just a house cat, the ginger feline had become a superb hunter, a feral terror, an efficient killer. She'd not long moved into the middle valley, and as she did, the birds there would know her by the fear she spread and call her by their ancient and feared name for such a demon; a Keere, a bringer of doom.

-0-

High above the destruction of Phil's bower a scout patrol of mytre were flying over the upper valley. Karnny and Waytsill flew close together in formation with one bird slightly in front of the other. Each scanned the sky around them and the trees below.

The cat hunched over the dead bowerbird as if protecting it from their powerful eyesight. However, under the ferns and small tree's foliage, the searching scout flight saw nothing and were soon flying on to explore other parts of the escarpment's side and upper valley.

Once they'd passed, the ginger feral cat was left to eat her prey in peace, in the wreckage of the once beautiful bower structure that was now a final monument to Phil's life of labour. All the cat thought was, *That was easy*.

2

A CAT COMES TO THE VALLEY

And the cat's in the cradle and the silver spoon
Little boy blue and the man on the moon
"When you comin' home, Dad?"
"I don't know when, but we'll get together then
You know we'll have a good time then"

Harry Chapin – "Cats in the Cradle" (1974)

THE CAT MOVED low and slow over the ground in the upper valley, where the valley creek began. It had never been this far down the valley before, and its caution was the result of months of living wild and by its own raw instincts as it transformed from domestic cat to efficient wild hunter. It's bright neat ginger fur had at first been a hinderance to hunting, although as time passed the cat's fur had become matted and dirty, helping it blend easily into the undergrowth and shadows of the low scrub of the upper valley.

Now as the cat eased forward nothing saw or heard its advance. The bower bird meal had been a bonus and the cat's tummy was still full as she carefully looked for a warm well-hidden place to sleep and digest her meal.

She could see two birds flying high above the valley. They were black and white coloured birds like the ones she'd seen on the escarpment a few days before. But she knew that if she stayed well hidden in the undergrowth, she would be safe from discovery. *Anyway*, she thought, *those birds are too small to bother me.*

She saw a tall gum tree stretching up into the sky before her. Its trunk bark was still black from the fire that occurred over a year before, but its roots must have been deep because the tree looked healthy and strong, with its branches heavy under a cascade of leaves. The sun's rays burst through in places and created a dappled mat across the exposed roots and fallen leaves at the base of the tree. The cat could see what looked like a safe warm place between two claw-like pale roots and she crept swiftly and silently forward to inspect the ground nest.

Perfect, she thought, as she hopped over one of the roots and into the sunlight between the root's limbs. A small bed of leaf litter lay prepared for her to rest on and in a very short time as the sun rose high above the tree, she was warm and cosy and most importantly, she felt safe. Hidden from any creatures that might pass idly by, and camouflaged by her matted, dirty coat as she lay on the bed of green, red, golden leaves.

As she slept, she dreamt about her life with the norzela in their norzela nest high on the escarpment. It was warm and cosy, she was well fed and cared for. But her instinct told her something wasn't right. That cats were not pets and despite her comforts her primal need was to fulfil her destiny as a hunter, as a killer and survivor in the wild. She purred softly as she slept, and a sense of satisfaction settled in her mind. Hunter, killer, survivor she repeated in her dream. Hunter, killer, survivor. This was who she was now. No more the ginger puss. No more the gentil house cat.

Egnaro's time, and darkness had become her domain. Elppa's time and lightness were her bedtime, her time to rest. Her wonderful lowlight vision meant few animals escaped her notice as she'd patrolled the upper escarpment, and it was from up there, high on the escarpment's side that she saw the lower valley, with its stream, and shady trees.

She'd seen that there were a few norzela nests too and she remembered that they often offered warm shelter, if she needed it. The lower valley looked like it also offered an excellent opportunity to hunt under the trees or in the open paddocks, or even by the road, where she knew that she could take advantage of roadkill, if other chances of a kill were scarce. *A golden land she,* thought in her dream. *The lower valley would become her domain. Her new home.*

Nothing disturbed her sleep, but as the sun sank in the east and the shadows grew, she became cold and was aware it was time to move again. She'd been lucky in her kill of the black bird high on the escarpment shelf, and with the silly dancing-singing bird near the bower, but she knew Egnaro's time was the best time to hunt, and night was only a few hours away. She stretched out her forelegs and arched her head and neck to look over the tree roots at her surroundings.

Nothing seemed to stir. She curved her back as she rose to her feet and stretched again. This time every muscle and tendon were stretched out. Even her claws popped free from their nest in her feet to scratch across the leaves of her bed. Then she jumped lightly on to one of the tree roots confidently exposing herself as she did. There she sat proudly licking her forepaws and rolling her paws over her ears and face, pampering and preening herself at her leisure.

A small lizard scurried across the tree's trunk until it stopped with a sudden shock. Seeing the cat it instantly ran up and then around the tree's trunk desperately trying to escape the evil it had encountered. She was still enjoying the delights of a full belly and after her long sleep she was not in the mood to hunt or to eat again so soon. She watched the lizard clammer away quickly as it disappeared around to the other side of the tree.

There will be other... better feasts tonight, she thought as she returned to her preening duties. The sun set lower, and darkness began to fill the glade around the tall tree near the small stream. *I'll follow the stream tonight,* she thought, knowing it was her highway into the heart of the lower valley. *But not yet. Not until Elppa has completely gone. Then I will explore further into my new domain.*

3

CHICKS

CORDELIA WATCHED the norzela leave their nest on the western side of the valley, a few days before the chicks hatched. The norzela spent the whole day loading what looked a lot like cages or boxes into the big car before they all got into a smaller car and followed the bigger one as it drove along the driveway and turned right onto the sealed road. Cordelia had an excellent vantage point as she sat on her nest and two eggs that she couldn't leave.

She was fascinated by the bustle and activity around the once quiet norzela nest. They haven't used the nest long, Cordelia thought. The nest had not long been rebuilt after the flood, but clearly the norzela family that had moved in were unhappy or had simply decided to move to a new nest. Cordelia didn't understand at all but couldn't help noticing the flurry of their departure.

As she watched, she sensed her eggs were approaching maturity and she could feel their arrival was imminent. However, they had still not hatched when another small car drove up and parked outside the abandoned norzela nest. This was followed by another massive car that came to a halt in the driveway of the norzela nest.

Soon a host of norzela were busy unloading what looked like the same boxes or cages onto the driveway and then carrying them into the norzela nest.

"New norzela are moving into the nest," Cordelia said to Barry as he returned to the nest with a fat grub for Cordelia to enjoy.

"Thanks Barry," Cordelia said as she took the grub and swallowed it in one gulp.

"The chicks will be here soon," Cordelia suggested as Barry slumped down into the nest, next to his partner. "Then you'll know fatigue my love," she said, mockingly, as she nuzzled her head into his neck.

Barry looked over the lip of the nest and watched the norzela for a moment.

"Look," he said, "they have a small dog." The dog was a Yorkshire Terrier or 'Yorkie' and it was no bigger than a moderately sized cat. It's long, grey, combed hair made it look like a wig on legs. Cordelia looked over the lip of the nest, its size reminded her of Bruce, the house dog from the sheep station. She wondered how her small dog friend was doing and if he missed her, as she missed him. Her mind drifted, back to the warm air and dry dust of the station. Thoughts of Gary, Trev and Sid, and even the norzela girl who had taken care of her, flashed into Cordelia's mind. A sadness overcame her for a moment.

Then she was aware again of Barry at her side, and she felt something under her belly; a sharp pecking feeling. "It's time," Cordelia said softly, "the eggs are cracking."

-0-

All thoughts of the new norzela, their small dog, and the activity at the norzela nest passed with the chick's arrival. Cordelia and Barry were delighted, and birds from all over the lower valley flew to offer their congratulations. The two willie-wagtail chicks that Cordelia had saved the day of the flood, and their father Olie, came to offer their best wishes and made an offer to help in any way with the new chick's care. The splendid fairy wrens flew up from the nest they had rebuilt by the new norzela nest to add their congratulations and offered to help with the new chick's care. Corselia was soon at the nest fussing and flapping about pecking at the broken pieces of egg and tossing them from the nest.

"Mother," Cordelia said, with mock annoyance, "I can manage, now give us some space before you accidently peck and clear one of the chicks from the nest."

"I am just trying to help, dear," Corselia said in her defence, "I am so overjoyed at their arrival, you and Barry are so lucky to have these chicks here in the very nest tree where you were born."

As Elppa passed, other mytre of the Valley Clan flew by to pay their respects or offer their thoughts and congratulations. Corxell and Karnny took time from one of their scout flights to drop in, before returning to their scouting duties.

"What will you call them?" Corxell asked before he left, taking to wing above their nest tree.

"You'll be the first to know," Cordelia called after him. Before looking at Barry and saying, "You know I hadn't given their names any thought."

"We can decide later, dear," Barry said. Adding, "I'll get some food for the chicks," as he prepared to take off.

"I'll come with you," Corselia offered, joining him in flight.

-0-

Just before ksud settled over the valley, Waytbill and Waytsill came to offer their good wishes.

"Sorry we are so late," Waytbill offered, as the two mytre came in, to land on a branch opposite Cordelia's nest.

"There was some commotion near the norzela park. The scouts thought they saw a cat near the elpitlum site we used after the flood," Waytsill said without thinking.

Waytbill shot him a tempered look, and added, "We joined them but couldn't see anything. I think they were mistaken… I'm sure it's nothing to worry about," Waytbill concluded. Adding, "Now let's see these new chicks of yours."

The chicks were squawking and crying out to be fed and Corselia and Barry had not yet returned to the nest. Cordelia looked alarmed and asked, "Are you sure there is no cat threat? A cat is the last thing we need in the valley." Cordelia knew that one of the biggest threats to mytre chicks was a cat and she was immediately alarmed.

"We saw no sign of a cat, no tracks, no kills, no sign at all. I think it was a false alarm." Cordelia had not sensed a cat in the valley, but she had been distracted by the chick's arrival and the norzela's coming and going from the norzela nest. Cordelia felt a fog had settled over her mind. An 'egg head' mind she had heard other mytre call the fuzziness that settles on the mind of a mytre while they sit on the nest. *This was no time to be fuzzy*, she thought. *I need to get out of the nest and feel the wind under my wings to blow the fuzziness away.*

The chicks' mouths were open wide and crying out to be fed and Waytbill and Waytsill soon saw Cordelia had enough to deal with without their presence.

"I'll keep an eye out with the valley scouts," Waytbill said, "Don't you worry, I'll keep an eye out over the valley, I'm sure it's nothing. Congratulations," he added before both visiting mytre dropped from the branch and took to wing.

-0-

Cordelia had been on the eggs a long time and her mind had indeed been preoccupied. Now the eggs had hatched she felt it was high time to fly again.

As soon as Barry returned to the nest, she watched him feed the chicks before saying, "I have to fly, Barry. I've been in the nest too long, my love."

Barry was taken aback.

"But the chicks have just hatched, I can fly and feed them and Corselia is helping. You rest," he protested.

"No…" Cordelia said sternly, before softening her tone, "no, love, I just need to stretch my wings, get my head free of the 'egg head' fog I feel. I can bring back some food, and we can share the work between us."

Barry recognised her feelings of frustration. He'd felt it himself when he'd been flightless on the tree stump in the forest for just one passing of Egnaro. *How must Cordelia be feeling after many passings of Egnaro and Elppa?* he thought.

"Be careful," Barry said, adding, "ksud is coming soon and you have not flown for a long while. Take care and come back soon. Your chick's and I need you."

Cordelia and Barry touched beaks softly and she closed her eyes as they embraced briefly, lifting their wings to wrap each other's face and heads.

"I'll not be long, love," she said softly, before stretching her wings and taking flight. She dived down through the branches of their nest tree and then, up into the growing gloom of the ksud sky. Cordelia flew high, higher even than the scout groups that flew each day over the valley. High above the valley, especially at dusk, she could bathe in the glory of her valley home and the setting of Elppa's light.

-0-

As she flew, she recalled Kratatora's sacrifice high on the escarpment ledge and wished she could have acted sooner to save her friend's life. It chilled her to very quill to think of how close they had come to losing the valley to the lizard horde and the evil Silas.

She thought too of the two malicious ravens that had been vanquished on the shelf, and it was only then that she remembered the cat that had skulked off with Obsidian in her mouth. *Could this be the same cat that has come to the valley,* Cordelia thought.

As she drifted on the breeze Cordelia felt that the valley seemed to have returned to the quiet home it had been after the fire. The various clans were now all united as members of the Valley Clan and talk or even mention of their former clan names seemed to have passed out of memory. Cordelia flew south to their border with the eucalypt forest. As she did, she searched the trees for Cal or Lathami, the two glossy black cockatoos they helped when their territory had been threatened by norzela developers. Cordelia had not spoken with them for a long time, but she knew they remained allies and firm friends.

As Cordelia turned away from the forest, she was reminded that it is only by helping our friends and allies that they will feel willing to return the favour. She could see in the distance that although parts of the eucalypt forest had been transformed into norzela parks and walking tracks, she knew that the glossy black cockatoo's territory was now safe and remained a secure and free habitat where the black birds could flourish. Although, she hadn't seen either of the black cockatoos, she wasn't worried as she knew that Cal and Lithami had a chick of their own and were likely busy caring for their own young.

Korzela's wind gusted from the south and blew Cordelia towards the sealed road that ran through the Valley Clan's land and skies. It was here, amongst a few tall gums that had survived the fire, that Waytjulia and Waytbill had established their nest, and they too were expecting chicks in the coming days. As Cordelia flew high on the breeze she could see the nest in the branches of the tall gum. Waytjulia was seated on her and Waytbill's nest, and she called out to Cordelia as she swooped low at speed past their tree.

She flew on past the nests Karnny and Corxell had established in a huge tree that had survived the fire and the flood in the very heart of the Valley Clan lands.

They had no mates yet and lived a sort of bachelor lifestyle, independent of the other birds of the clan. But each had also taken on responsibility for the wide arial patrols above the clan lands while the partnered mytre tended their eggs and chicks. Cordelia noted that neither were in their nests or on the bows of their tree as she passed, and she sensed too late Karnny's attack from above.

"Got yer," Karnny cried as he arrowed past her right wing before pulling up and swinging round to fly parallel to Cordelia. He was suddenly joined by Corxell, Cordelia's older and bigger brother. Both young male birds had grown into hansom mytre with shiny black and bright white plumage. As the three birds flew in a line, with Karnny and Corxell on each side of Cordelia, she couldn't help but be impressed with their hunting and patrol skills.

"Where did you come from?" Cordelia asked in a state of genuine shock.

"Above and with the setting sun behind us," Karnny explained with pride.

"Well, I can see the Valley Clan will have no need to fear a surprise attack any time soon with you out on patrol," Cordelia said sincerely.

"How are the chicks?" Corxell asked.

"Hungry," Cordelia called back before dropping low and turning toward the norzela nest, west of the tall ghost gum that had been her former Cor clan nest tree and her home all her life. "And their father will be expecting me as I'm sure he'll be hungry too… bye boys," she called as she dropped lower towards the area of her own nest tree.

Karnny and Corxell swung around and turned back to their own nest tree in the centre of the valley.

Cordelia suddenly turned and started to climb into the growing darkness as Elppa set. She flew higher, up toward the escarpment cliffs. The final rays of Elppa's light made the cliff face turn red and golden and stand out above the valley. She knew it was unwise to fly alone, but she had something she wanted to see.

She flapped quickly and was soon over the high escarpment shelf, where the battle had taken place. The cage she knew was gone, and there was nothing to signal or mark the scale of the battle that had taken place there. *It looks peaceful and quiet*, she thought.

Then she spiralled down to the trees and bushes at the foot of the escarpment. She dare not land, but she flew quietly and swiftly between the branches and fern fronds as the darkness enveloped the upper valley. It was hard to see but as her eyes adjusted to the dim light she saw the destroyed bower. *No bird would leave a bower in this state*, she thought, as she flew back and around to get a better look at the destruction of the bower bird's nest. In spite of her better instincts, she landed before the gathered stones and blue trinkets at the mouth of the torn nest. She knew at once, *A cat did this*.

4

CHICKADEE

Every little swallow, every chickadee
Every little bird in the tall oak tree
The wise old owl, the big black crow
Flap-a their wings, singin', "Go bird go"

Bobby Day – 'Rockin' Robin' (1958)

BARRY AND CORDELIA were flying more than they had ever flown before. The two small chicks needed constant attention, and they each relished the job of finding food to feed their chicks. Each took off and returned to the nest with food, flying sortie after sortie to keep the bellies of their two chicks full. Corselia and Corxell and the small fairy wren and the young willie-wagtails were there to help, and their input was invaluable, but Cordelia and Barry were still exhausted with the effort of searching for food, and flying back and forth with grasshoppers, grubs, worms, insects, and anything they could scrounge from the valley.

A number of other mated mytre pairs of the valley, including Waytbill and Waytjulia also had hatchlings and the combined effort of feeding the new chicks, meant Cordelia needed to wait until all the young birds had fledged before she could call an elpitlum. Everyone knew that the lizards, their leader Silas and the two malicious ravens had been vanquished and few in the valley suspected another danger might be imminent.

But Cordelia was less sure, and with each passing of Elppa she began to feel the dread and unease that she'd felt before the lizard invasion.

She told Barry about her concerns and about the bower bird nest that she'd found destroyed. "I can feel it. There is a keere thing coming to the valley again. A cat is loose in the middle valley and it's coming here." Cordelia spoke with the clarity of one who'd seen it all play out before her eyes.

"But what can we do now, half the mytre of the valley have chicks, chicks that we desperately need, chicks that will help grow the Valley Clan's strength, chicks that we love and chicks that can't fight or fly, even if a cat comes."

"All the more reason to call an elpitlum and discuss what we can do," Cordelia protested.

"We have the scouting patrols now, they'll watch over us and warn us if there is a keere killer on the loose," Barry reassured her.

"But what if they can't find the cat? What if it comes with Egnaro's glow when our watchers are resting?" They whispered quietly as they sat on a branch above their nest, while Cordelia's mother, Corselia sat with the chicks.

"Hope is no defence if we don't even know our enemy," Cordelia said, before adding, "I asked the scout patrols to search specifically for a cat coming from the north, in the direction of the escarpment, but so far they haven't seen anything."

"Which could mean there is nothing to find…" Barry began.

"…or the cat is too clever for our searchers?" Cordelia suggested, as she started to feel exasperated.

"Trust the patrols," Barry began, "You have given us a warning, now trust to the skill of the scouts to warn us if a cat really is coming to the valley. You trained us well," Barry said kindly.

"But you and the others were trained for an air invasion, not for a cat attack," Cordelia said softly, adding, "Cats are different. They're cruel, ruthless and totally focused on one thing… death. Death regardless of need. They hunt to kill not just for food.

They have no soul. No connection to others and no heart. They cannot be reasoned with, and they love the thrill of the kill."

Barry reeled in shock, his eyes widened, and his beak dropped open. He knew that a cat could be dangerous, and that they hunted alone and often once Egnaro was awake, but he had no idea about their lust to kill at any price. He was immediately alert to the significance of the danger Cordelia identified.

"Well, we should send up two search teams each day and call an elpitlum as soon as possible," Barry said with a tone of urgency. "I'll go and talk with Waytbill and Waytjulia now. As you said, we have to meet as soon as possible. You talk with Karnny, Corxell and Waytsill and see if they can find another scout so they can fly patrols at both nwad and ksud."

Cordelia was stunned at his reaction but pleased too that he'd responded so positively to her message. "I agree," she found herself saying, "but it must wait until nwad. We have the chicks to feed and Corselia will want to go to her own nest after chick-sitting since nwod." Neither were happy, but they each knew they needed to wait until Elppa's return to talk with the others.

-0-

The cat moved stealthily through the undergrowth at night. Stopping every few metres to crouch and listen to the plethora of sounds around her as she made no sound at all. She could hear insects calling and buzzing, birds chirping their final ksud calls, and in the near distance she could hear a willie-wagtail singing on a low branch.

As it sang it twitched its tail back and forth in a dance before Egnaro's glow.

The ginger cat crept up from the creek and below what she assumed was a dam above her. The trees were sparce and the bushes only just coming back to maturity after the fire and flood's destruction. As well as the twitter of the willie-wagtail near the norzela nest, she could hear the tug, tug, tug of a generator that operated a pump in the pump house near the lower slope of the dam. *Good*, she thought, *this will help me hide as I approach.*

Olie, the willie-wagtail, was lamenting the loss of his mate in the flood. They had survived the fire, but the flood had claimed her life when she refused the offer of Cordelia's help. Now, in the peace of the valley, Olie sang as he'd done to his partner Marrion, whenever Egnaro's full glow blessed the valley. He was perched on a low branch of a slender gum tree hoping to sing out clearly under Egnaro's glow.

He raised his voice to the bright orb and found himself caught and choked with emotion as he remembered his partner.

"Marrion," he sang, "Marrion, my love." His voice was a high staccato that pierced the night. The pump by the dam chugged on, offering a low constant rhythm to accompany his high tone. He didn't hear the cat's approach, and the cat didn't see the two smaller willie-wagtails perched near their nest in a bush by the new norzela nest. Each had come to the fringes of the bush to watch their father sing to his former partner, their mother, Marrion.

They saw the cat a moment before it struck, and even their warning cries failed to save their father's life. In a flash the cat had the small bird in its claws, pulled down and pinned to the ground, as Olie panted and flapped in shock and panic. It was over quickly. The small bird faced death with dignity and was soon held tightly by the vile feral killer.

His children, who had survived the flood, the lizard invasion, and who had been saved by Cordelia, Barry, and Corselia now sat in horror as they witnessed their father's death under the claws of the cat. Both instinctively flew to their father's aid, flying quickly at the cat's face and head, trying desperately to avenge their father and distract the cat.

"Foolish chicks," the cat called as he struck out with one claw, while holding Olie under the other. The first chick to attack was quickly snatched from the air and the cat now looked to have two small birds for supper.

The second of Olie's chicks darted in to attack the cat and help save his kin, but the assault was futile and too late.

Olie called out with his last breath, "Fly away, Chickadee, save yourself," before the cat twisted her claws and silenced her father. Now the cat had a captive bird under each paw and could do little else but try and snap at the willie-wagtail with its teeth.

"Let them go, let them go," the small, distraught bird called as it buzzed and flashed in and away from the feral monster's face. "Father," Chickadee called through a flood of tears, "Father." But she heard no reply, and she dashed in at the cat once again.

"Are they your kin, bird?" the cat asked cruelly as it snapped at the broken-hearted pest. Feeling content with the double kill and not wanting to alarm any other creatures, the cat gathered up her prey and dashed away, quickly into the undergrowth above the dam.

"Come back, come back," the remaining willie-wagtail, Chickadee, called lamentably through her sobs. 'Come back…" But the cat and her now dead kin were gone into the gloom of the valley's underbrush. Summoning all her courage Chickadee decided to follow the vile feral cat, thinking that, if I can't defeat it in a fight, I could at least learn more about it and help warn my valley friends.

5

NEW OWNERS

And I know I'm right
For the first time in my life
That's why I tell you
You'd better be home soon

Crowded House – 'Better Be Home Soon' (1988)

THE PEOPLE WHO moved into the house on the western side of the valley, near the ghost gum that was now Cordelia's own nest tree, were Tran and Val, and their teenage daughter, Bree. Tran had long held a desire to live in a rural property and the small newly re-build home with a few hectares of land and a small, re-established dam had been too much to resist. The property had an established chicken coop, and his hope was to plant some fruit trees, a veggie patch and flowers, and maybe even build a beehive and gather honey.

The people who'd rebuilt the home simply couldn't adjust to life on the land after facing the fire and flood in such quick succession. They'd rebuilt, and made it comfortable, but only so they could sell up and move on. Tran and Val had put in a very reasonable offer and were totally shocked that the old owners were very keen to sell and be gone so quickly.

Bree hated the idea of the move.

"What about my friends in town?" she'd protested, "How will I keep in touch with them now?"

Val had solved the problem when she offered Bree a puppy as compensation for the move. Bree agreed almost at once and Val felt Bree's friends would have been hurt to hear their friendship was only as valuable as a small Yorkshire Terrier puppy.

"A yorkie," Bree exclaimed excitedly, "I'll call him Jock," she said beaming.

"He'd better not upset my chickens," Val said. "Those 11 hens and that rooster will keep us in eggs and I'll be very upset if they are scared off laying because of a small dog, no matter how cute it is." So it was that Tran, Val, Bree, Jock and Val's egg laying 11 chickens, and one rooster moved into the newly refurbished home below the dam on the western side of the Valley Clan's valley.

The chicken coop was a new addition to the land behind the norzela nest, having been built only after the fire. Cordelia flew over it and was amazed to see a collection of captive birds scratching about behind the wire and wood of the coop.

"What sort of bird are they?" she asked Barry. Barry was delighted that this was something he knew about, "Ah," he said proudly feeling pleased that he knew something Cordelia clearly did not. "These are birds called chicken or fowl. They live in coexistence with norzela, and they exchange eggs for food."

"It sounds barbaric," Cordelia exclaimed.

"Why don't they try to escape and fly away?" Cordelia asked.

"Because these birds cannot fly," he replied. Cordelia recalled another flightless bird she had encountered at the station. Bruce, the housedog, had talked about a massive bird called an 'emu'. Then she remembered that her mother Corselia had also told her about them. They had grown too fat to fly, and she also called them 'emu'. But these small birds were not too fat to fly. Surely Barry was mistaken.

"They live in the cage and provide eggs for the norzela,' Barry repeated. Adding, "It must be a sad life being a bird without the gift of flight."

Cordelia and Barry continued to watch the new developments at the norzela nest as they flew sortie after sortie in search of food for their two small mytre chicks. Corselia, who was helping feed the small brood, soon noticed that the norzela boys had gone and seemed to have been replaced by one norzela girl. *I hope she isn't as mean as the norzela boys,* she thought. She told Cordelia of her father's heroics in chasing away the two scallywag norzela boys when Cordelia was just a chick. Barry said, "I'd do the same if any norzela tried to throw rocks at my nest tree."

"My nest tree, indeed," said Cordelia with a smile, and a mock dig at Barry.

"Oh…I meant our nest tree, dear," he said hoping to recapture his faux pas.

They had all observed the three new norzela and the chickens and the small hairy dog and Cordelia suddenly said, "I might go down there now and see if I can make friends with the little dog." Adding, "Any ally is a good ally." Then without more discussion, she hopped over to a branch ready to take off. Ksud was approaching and she knew there was serious work to do with Elppa's light, but she took this opportunity to approach the dog and build an alliance ahead of the coming elpitlum and the possible confrontation with a cat.

-0-

Cordelia landed on a low fence that surrounded the re-laid patch of front lawn. The wire fence was left over from an attempt to keep the previous owners two norzela boys off the lawn. It failed, as Cordelia had seen the boys running and kicking a football on it on multiple occasions, before the boys and their family moved out. Cordelia liked the boys running on the lawn, it helped loosen the soil and even expose insects or grubs. After the boys had gone inside, she often flew down to the lawn in search of food.

The boys where gone now and she hopped down from the wire fence and landed on the lawn to strut about pecking here and there in the lawn or soil. Cordelia had seen the young dog pretending to be asleep as it lay near a small kennel. It reminded Cordelia of the kennels the yard-dog had slept in at the station, but this dog did not seem to be tied or chained up. The dog slowly opened its eyes and waited until Cordelia had her back to the kennel, before darting out across the lawn in an attempt to catch the intruding bird. As Jock ran his little legs raced as fast as they could go, although he still looked to Cordelia like a short hairy mop had escaped from a bucket and was free to dance across the lawn. Cordelia waited until the last moment before lifting into the sky and coming to rest on the norzela nest's guttering.

"Nearly had me," Cordelia called down to the small dog.

"Jock," he shouted back, barking as loudly as he could. "Jock is my name, and this is my lawn, you should stay away. I am a dog of the yorkie clan, and I am here to guard this yard from intruders."

From the safety of the guttering Cordelia called down, "What a noble and efficient guard you are, and you are so very handsome too."

"I know," Jock replied in an avalanche of conceit.

"Do you live here now, Jock of the yorkie clan?" Cordelia asked politely, adding, "I am Cordelia of the Valley Clan, my home is over there in a tall tree. We are neighbours it seems, and I have come to welcome you to the valley."

"The valley?" Jock barked.

"Yes, all the land and sky about here, and by the creek is the Valley Clan land and sky and we are delighted to have a neighbour and friend who is so handsome and strong living in the new norzela nest."

"Why would I need to be friends with a mytre?" Jock asked. "I've never had a bird as a friend, before."

"That's a shame," Cordelia began, "I have been friends with many dogs, and they have all profited from our confederacy."

"What dog? There is no other dog here," Jock shot back.

"All the more reason to be friends with a mytre," Cordelia said, cleverly. Before adding, "My other dog friends were on a sheep station a long way from here. But we were very good friends, and they were some of the most handsome and clever dogs I had ever known." Cordelia paused and walked along the guttering a little before saying, "I can see you are beautiful, but are you a clever dog?"

"I am," barked Jock, loudly.

"Then I will set you a test and if you pass it, we can be friends," Cordelia suggested.

"What sort of test?" Jock demanded.

"Well," Cordelia began, "you and I will become firm friends until you can catch one of my tail feathers. For if you are so clever as to catch one of my tail feathers, I fear you will be too clever to be a friend of mine. However, in return, as your friend, I will warn you of danger should it come, help you if you are lost or alone, and bring you food if you have been neglected by your owners and become hungry."

"So, we are already friends…" Jock speculated.

"As long as you don't catch one of my tail feathers," Cordelia clarified.

"Splendid," Jock barked in delight, adding, "Here let me try now… come down to the lawn and let me try to catch your tail feathers now."

"See I knew you were a smart dog, Jock," Cordelia said, "Right away you tried to trick me into coming down to play, knowing you are faster and smarter than I am."

"Yes, I am fast," Jock replied, before bursting into a dash around the lawn's perimeter. Jock was delighted to have an audience, and he ran a half a dozen laps of the lawn at a terrific speed before collapsing near his small kennel with his tongue lolling out of the side of his panting mouth.

"Wonderful," Cordelia said, as she flew down to stride about on the lawn.

"Can I come back and play another time, Jock?" She asked as she pecked at the soil and listened for grubs under the grass roots. Jock looked up at Cordelia as she moved slowly before him on the lawn, barely a greyhound's stride from his kennel. Jock could hardly bark, and he gave up the idea of trying to catch one of Cordelia's tail feathers today.

"Come back any time, mate," Jock managed to pant, "any time." Cordelia took a few more strides and then lifted into the sky, content that she and Jock would become good friends.

-0-

Chickadee was waiting in Cordelia and Barry's ghost gum nest when she returned from tormenting Jock. Cordelia returned in a light mood and was about to tell Barry all about her encounter with Jock when she saw the dishevelled and exhausted looking willie-wagtail in the nest. The small bird was laying on one side with a gash across her face and wing. Barry was tending her wounds and had called for Corselia's help. Corselia arrived only moments before Cordelia, and she too was in a state of shock at the condition of the small bird.

"What's occurred?" Cordelia exclaimed as she bent to look over at the willie-wagtail's injuries.

"Step back. Give her some air,' Barry said gently, as he lifted the injured birds wing into a more comfortable position.

"Has there been a fight? Are the lizards back?" Cordelia asked as she struggled to comprehend the tragedy. *Or is it the cat?* she thought. She had suspected it was close by.

Corselia asked Barry to hop aside, so she could take care of the quivering willie-wagtail. He didn't hesitate and moved quickly to Cordelia's side so he could comfort her instead. They embraced quickly and tightly.

"She flew here only a short while before you returned," Barry explained, adding, "She's been flying all through the passage of Elppa and she has a dreadful and sad story for us all. But I think

29

she needs to rest now and regain her strength. I can tell you the little I know, but she must be allowed to rest now." Barry's voice sounded sad, and his tone rang of despair and disaster.

"Let her rest," he repeated solemnly, before whispering, "I'll tell you what I know." Corselia moved Cordelia and Barry's crying chicks to one side of the nest and asked them to be quiet. At the same time, she placed some galah-down she'd taken from near the dam and used it to cushion the injured Chickadee's head. Within a moment, Chickadee was asleep as exhaustion overtook her. The two chicks remained quiet, and Barry whispered the little he knew to the other adult mytre in the nest. He spoke quickly and quietly. "Olie is dead and so is the other of his chicks." Corselia and Cordelia recoiled in shock.

"How?" Cordelia called.

"No..." Corselia gasped.

"Chickadee here, only just survived, and she decided to follow her attacker so she could report back on the extent of the threat." Barry paused and looked from Corselia to Cordelia, before saying, "Cordelia you were right. There's a cat in the valley, and it's causing a wave of devastation and terror that Lord Kratt and the lizards could only imagine."

6

THE STORY OF CORDELIA'S LOVE FOR HER CHICKS

Love, love changes everything: hands and faces, earth and sky.
Love, love changes everything: how you live and how you die.
Love can make the summer fly, or a night seem like a lifetime.
Yes, love, love changes everything, now I tremble at your name.
Nothing in the world will ever be the same.

Andrew Lloyd Webber – 'Love Changes Everything' (1989)

BARRY AND CORDELIA flew to the other mytres of the Valley Clan as soon as Elppa had risen. They didn't even wait for the Elppa chorus, so anxious were they to bring the rest of the clan to the elpitlum. Some refused to go even after they had heard the tail of what had occurred to Chickadee, her sister, and Olie. Others concerned for protocol refused to attend immediately and wanted to wait until a formal discussion had occurred, a formal agenda had been agreed and until after they had sung to Elppa.

Even Waytbill was reluctant, and it took all of Cordelia's wit to get him to see that there was no point in having a scout patrol or information about imminent danger if they were incapable of acting on it. Many of the mytre still with chicks in the nest simply said they couldn't afford to stop their work of finding food.

They said that their chick's hunger couldn't wait, Others were too preoccupied with petty domestic duties, and they couldn't give up time for a 'non-existent threat'.

31

"I can't stop my job as provider for my chicks on the word of a twittering willie-wagtail," one said.

"Prove there's a cat and I'll come immediately, but, I can't see anything here but panic and hot air," another suggested, before returning to hunt for grubs and insects for his young.

Cordelia and Barry were disappointed and almost beside themselves with anxiety. This just made some of the valley mytre less inclined to listen to them. They could see their fellow mytre's perspective but felt few of the valley mytre could comprehend the impending danger.

"We may feel the same if we hadn't heard Chickadee's story firsthand," Barry suggested.

"And if I had not foreseen the cat's approach, and seen the destruction at the bower for myself," Cordelia added.

Still, they flew to the elpitlum site and waited for others to arrive. In the end only about half the valley mytre came to the elpitlum. Most were young and unmatched, but all were fired up with the knowledge that Cordelia must have something worthwhile to say, given the urgency with which they were called to gather.

The new Valley Clan elpitlum site was where the elpitlum had been before the flood. The logs were gone, washed down the valley with the waters, but the area was still a suitable grassy clearing, away from over hanging tree branches and bare of shrubs and bushes. The Valley Clan birds gathered in a rough circle and waited for Cordelia to speak. All the mytre were anxious and they flapped and squawked making gestures at each other as they waited, and it took a while for them to come to order.

"Quiet now, listen everyone," Cordelia called above the din.

"Wait," Waytbill called out more loudly, bringing the gathered mytre to silence.

"I know Cordelia has called the elpitlum for an urgent matter, but I want to start by acknowledging Kratatora's death on the escarpment. I think we should start by singing him into the Great

Flock of Elppa. Something that should have occurred many passings of Elppa ago."

A number of mytre called their agreement and one called out, "It's been too long, it's time to honour the great warrior of the Kratt clan."

"No… there's no time," Cordelia shouted above the chatter. Her frustration had grown with the repeated delays, and she shouted, "No…we have an urgent issue to discuss." She sounded almost hysterical at this point, and many mytre started to step away from her, as if her distress was catchy.

"You would want us to sing you into the Great Flock, I'm sure," one of the gathered mytre said sarcastically.

"I would if I were dead," Cordelia called back, "and that's more likely if we don't act soon." She felt herself losing her temper. Barry reached a wing out to comfort and settle her anxiety. Cordelia could sense that her frustration and fear were pushing her argument onto deaf ears. Like sea birds blown by Korzela (the God of wind) onto the rocks. A young mytre called out, "allow us to sing Kratatora into the Great Flock as a mark of our respect, before you bring another disaster to our door."

"This valley is cursed," another mytre called out, adding, "the Kratt invasion, the fire, the flood, the lizard attack… now what has Cordelia 'the great' brought to our nests?"

A few mytre sniggered at the bird's wit, but Waytbill snapped back at the dissenters quickly, "Cordelia has risked her life more than once for the valley and the Valley Clan. She is my friend, and I'm sorry I have not listened to her today. I can see now that something significant is coming. We are lucky to have a bird with Cordelia's gifts living with us."

Corxell, Karnny, and Waytsill called in support of the older, wiser bird. As the chorus settled, Waytbill turned to Cordelia and bowed low.

"I'm sorry, Cordelia, please tell us of the threat you for see."

"There is a threat coming. A cat of great malice is coming to the valley; indeed, it may already be here. But I understand your need to sing Kratatora into the Great Flock of Elppa. He was also my friend. I was there on the escarpment, where he was savagely killed, and we should celebrate his spirit as he flies with Elppa's flock." Cordelia knew this was important to any mytre and it was indeed too long since Kratatora's passing for them to sing her into the Great Flock of Elppa. She also knew that this would be a good way to help her relax, discard her frustration and take a breath before passing on worse news.

Barry placed a gentle wing on his partner's shoulder. "You start us, my dear," he whispered.

She stepped into the centre of the gathered mytre and began to sing, loudly and with great heart. Barry joined in soon after, as did, Waytbill, Corxell, Karnny, and Waytsill. Soon all the gathered mytre were lifting their voices in a *quardle oodle ardle wadle doodle*, singing of their friend and clan mytre companion.

"He had the idea for the scouting patrols," Karnny cried out.

"He tried to fight the great lizard, Silas," Barry lamented.

"He killed many lizards in the lizard battle," Waytsill sang.

"*Quardle oodle ardle wadle doodle, doodle wadle ardle, oodle*," they chorused as one, (Fly with the Great Flock, may the wind lift your spirit into the embrace of our great ancestors.)

Cordelia had started the lament, and it was Cordelia whose soft clear voice finished the last of the chorus. Their carolling had reached into the breezes of the valley and birds nesting in the great trees of the valley clearly heard their testament to Kratatora. Many mytre, laying with their chicks or out foraging for them, joined in, as the song echoed up and down the valley.

Even the new norzela in their nest heard the uplifting chorus and Tran and Val stopped their work to listen.

"Never heard that before," Tran said.

"Is that the magpies singing?" Val asked unsure.

"Yer...beautiful isn't it," Tran declared.

At the elpitlum, the mood remained low, sombre almost, as the mytre refocused on the news Cordelia and Barry had come to tell them. Calmer now and sure of what she needed to say, Cordelia soon passed on her message to all the Valley Clan gathered at the elpitlum. Most were shocked at the impending threat coming to the valley and at the death of the small willie-wagtails. Cordelia described what she and Chickadee had seen in the middle valley below the escarpment and of the approach of the cat. Some of the mytre remembered the domestic cat who had terrorised the old Kar clan before Lord Krat's arrival.

"Lord Krat had driven the cat off," one of the former Kratt clan members called out. "We can do it again," they proposed optimistically.

"That was a domestic nest bound cat, a terror I am sure but nothing like the evil that stalks the middle valley now," Cordelia suggested. Cordelia raised her wings and beat them as she spoke, "I've seen a destroyed bower and Chickadee told us that she had seen dead birds strewn across the valley floor, dead lizard, dead mammals, rats and mice, small native mice, and quoll, and even a kookaburra and a bush turkey. All killed not just for food, but for pleasure, for sport, for the joy of a kill."

"This is the evil that is about to descend on the valley," Barry said, "and our chicks are not safe unless we can find a way to defeat the vile cat." Barry and the others at the elpitlum suddenly turned as a high pitch cry rang out across the valley.

"That's Corselia's cry," Cordelia said suddenly afraid.

-0-

Corselia had agreed to stay with Cordelia and Barry's two chicks and look after the still sleeping Chickadee. The chicks were hungry, they were always hungry, but Corselia had told them they would have to wait until their parents returned before they could be fed. They protested and squawked waking Chickadee, before Corselia said, "I will tell you all a story while we wait for your mother and father to return. Chickadee come and rest at my side and I'll tell you the story of Cordelia's love for her children."

"This is also the story of how the Great Flock of Elppa started and how Cordelia's sacrifice began a mytre tradition. Now settle down and no more crying out for food, be patient young ones."

Corselia began, as all good stories do with, "Once upon a wing... all birds were content to be free to bring up their young any way they saw fit. Elppa rose and fell and neither Elppa nor Egnaro felt any need to interfere with how parents raised their children. One day though, the Lord Elppa noticed that Cordelia the Great had not risen to sing at his nwad chorus.

"'Why were you not singing to celebrate my blessings, Cordelia the Great?' the Lord asked. "I was with my chicks Lord Elppa, they require constant attention so they will be safe and grow. Feeding them is a constant duty and today, I was too busy with my brood to stop for my Elppa carolling.'

"'Too busy, too busy...' the Lord of day and warmth fumed incredulously.

"'I am not too busy to rise for you each day. I am not too busy to shed warmth across the world for all the creatures and plants. No... this is an insult.'

"Cordelia responded politely, 'But my chicks are young and fragile, they need constant attention, food and warmth. I'm their mother, and as you have responsibilities for the light, warmth and heat of the world, I am responsible for my chick's warmth and welfare. Forgive me Lord, I will not neglect you again.'

"'No...' the Lord Elppa replied angrily, 'you will not forget, because I will take your chicks as punishment for your disrespect. Tomorrow, when I return, I will take your younglings and banish them to the sky, to start a mytre flock of my own that I might command, away from you so you have no distraction or excuse not to carol and sing when I arrive each day.'

"'No! Lord, please. I was only doing what any good mother would do. Caring for my chicks. I'm sorry Lord, please... don't take my chicks.'

"'It's too late, I have spoken,' the Lord Elppa, boomed. 'I will be back tomorrow for your young. Now say your 'good-byes' and prepare for my wrath.'

"Cordelia was distraught and gripped with fear and dread. She couldn't lose her brood, but she never gave up hope that she would find a solution, and as she searched for food for her chicks, she asked advice from different forest creatures. First, she approached the quoll, and asked, 'Wise quoll, how do you hide your young from the Lord Elppa?' The quoll replied that she had a pouch. 'I can hide my young in my pouch and still hunt for food while I carry my young with me. Lord Elppa cannot see them, and I cause him no offence.' Cordelia thought about her reply then thanked the quoll for her help.

"Next Cordelia the Great came across a wombat. She asked the wombat how she cared for her young and hid them from Lord Elppa?

"'Oh, I have a burrow, underground, Lord Elppa can't see me in my burrow, and as I mostly come out at night, I only need to celebrate with Egnaro. My young are safe from Elppa's wrath underground.' Cordelia thanked the wombat and continued her search. Next, she came across a Tasmanian devil, and again Cordelia asked how she cared for her young and hid them from Elppa's wrath.

"'I don't much care for Elppa,' the devil began, 'but I live in a den during the day, and I also have a pouch for my young when they are only small. So even if Elppa does see me he will not see my young. However, I have one other defence if the Lord Elppa should come too close or show any interest in my young, I can scream like a banshee, and he will stay away, I'm sure.' The Tasmanian devil showed Cordelia what she meant and screamed at an alarming volume until Cordelia could take no more and flew home to her chicks with their meal. She felt sad, defeated, none of the animals had helped and nwad was approaching.

"Suddenly a small willie-wagtail landed near her nest. Cordelia explained her situation and expressed her belief that this was a problem she could not solve with her wit or cunning, tricks or intellect.

"The willie-wagtail, twisted and bobbed on a branch near her nest and said, "I can offer this one piece of advice if you will hear me, Cordelia the wise?

"'I will listen," Cordelia said, genuinely glad to be receiving what she hoped was helpful advice.

"The willie-wagtail began, 'This may not be a problem for your wit or cunning, tricks or intellect, this may be a problem that only love can solve. A mother's love is stronger than any tree trunk, more powerful than any mountain stream and more enduring that Elppa or Egnaro. Your love for your chicks is a power even Elppa cannot overcome.' As she finished speaking the willie-wagtail flitted into the air and flew away, like smoke on the breeze. Cordelia thought long and hard about what the little twittering visitor had said. As she thought, she drew her two chicks in close to her side, providing them with warmth in the cool nwad air. *A mother's love is stronger than any tree trunk, more powerful than any mountain stream and more enduring that Elppa or Egnaro*, Cordelia thought.

"Suddenly Elppa broke over the eastern horizon and in a booming voice called to Cordelia for her chicks to be surrendered.

"'No... Lord, you are wise and powerful I know. I'm sorry I missed singing at the nwad chorus, and I will never miss another. But you cannot have my chicks. Leave them, they are innocent. Take my life in their place. I will serve you well in my afterlife. Take me Lord and spare my chicks.' Cordelia spoke clearly and with the conviction of a mother's love. Lord Elppa was stunned. He had not expected to see a sacrifice like this. He had never been a mother, and he struggled to comprehend the surrender of her life for her chicks.

"'You love them, don't you?' he said softly. 'I see that now.' Cordelia bowed her head and stood over the two chicks in her nest, saying again, 'Please Lord Elppa take me, take my life. I will serve you well Lord.'

"The Lord Elppa looked kindly on Cordelia. She had already served him well in many tasks and labours. Now, seeing her willingness to sacrifice everything for her young, his heart softened. He called out again, 'But I had pledged to take your chicks to start my own flock in the sky to command, and I still plan to build my Great Flock. However, given your wish that I take your life instead of your chicks, I will accept your offer. But I will only take it when your time has come. Not now.

"Although, I will hold you to your pledge. When you die, you will be the first mytre in my Great Flock. You will lead my flock in the sky and gather in all the greatest and most worthy mytre so that my flock becomes the greatest and most brilliant mytre clan of all. The Great Flock of Elppa, with Cordelia the brave, the wise, the forgiving... and the loving leading it. I have spoken,' he said finally.

"Cordelia bowed low then reached her head high in a chorus of, *quardle oodle ardle waddle doodle.* In celebration of Lord Elppa's compassion and wisdom."

Corselia finished the story and looked at the chicks. She was sure each was asleep, comfortable and warm at her right flank. Then Corselia looked at Chickadee. Immediately she saw the terror on her face. Chickadee was looking over Corselia shoulder into the leaves on the tree branches.

"You followed me, bird," the cat snarled, "Your sister and father, were delicious, far sweeter than a brown rat, or feather covered kookaburra... now stay still and I'll make it quick." With that the cat bounced into the nest and tried to get a paw on the little willie-wagtail. Corselia crowed and squawked as loudly as she could.

"Fly," Corselia called, "fly little one." She knew the two chicks were too young to fledge and all she could do was fight off the savage intruder. Corselia turned quickly on the cat stabbing it several times on the head with her sharp beak. The cat ducked, but in the confines of the nest all she could do was receive the blows and try to stretch out with her forepaws aiming to scratch the large mytre. Corselia was a veteran fighter, and she was soon up on her feet kicking out and pecking savagely at the cat.

"Move to another branch," she called to the chicks, "higher up the tree, away from her claws." The chicks had never left the nest, and their fear was palpable as they stretched their stumpy wings and waddled uneasily across the lip of the nest and out onto a branch behind Corselia. However, the cat had not climbed all the way up the nest tree to come away empty pawed.

"Now the little bird has flown, I'll take one of your chicks then," the cat said snidely, as it ducked and parried Corselia's blows. Then it reached a strong forepaw out and scratched Corselia across the face. It was a brutal blow and Corselia reeled back unsteadily on her legs. Corselia's attack came to a halt as she tried to regain her balance.

The cat struck again. This time she sank her teeth into Corselia's shoulder, causing her to cry out in pain and distress. She collapsed into the bottom of the nest and was soon aware, even through her pain, that the cat was standing over her with its teeth ready to take her life. She tried to move but one wing was badly damaged and would not respond to her wishes, her other was pinned under the cat's left foot and claws.

"First you, then the chicks," the cat said triumphantly. Then, suddenly, Chickadee flapped into the cat's face, pecking where she could and distracting the terror so the cat couldn't deliver the fatal blow or bite. Then Cordelia, who had flown speedily back from the elpitlum, flew into the cat's flank winding it and knocking it from the nest. The cat was caught completely off guard, and it fell from the nest, falling about three body lengths until it landed paws up on an outstretched tree branch. Cordelia flew at it again, flapping and pecking with all her might.

"Those are my chicks," Cordelia cried, adding, "back off you ginger bitch." She had never felt so angry so enraged and so powerful. Corxell also joined the attack by diving and swooping the cat as it left the nest tree. The cat sensed the arrival of other mytre and soon saw the wisdom of retreat.

"I'll be back for you all," the cat cried, crouching low on the branch, before it jumped down to a lower limb and then another before scurrying away towards the norzela nest along the gravel driveway. Cordelia and Corxell harassed the cat as it fled along the driveway, although Cordelia soon returned to the nest tree to see what damage had been caused and to see if the chicks and Corselia were safe.

Corselia had saved the chicks, but at a dreadful cost. Her shoulder and wing looked to have been badly mauled and the scratch on her face would leave a life-long scar. She'd been helped to her feet, but she swooned and swayed and needed Cordelia's help to stay upright. The two chicks came back into the nest and were embraced by Barry who helped them calm down. Then they saw Chickadee. She was on the ground at the bottom of the nest tree. The cat's final blow had caught her across the chest and sent her spinning down, to crash on the ground far below.

Barry and Cordelia flew down to assess the small willie-wagtail's wounds, but the little hero had died in her final assault on the cat. Corselia was badly injured, and while the two chicks were traumatised it had been the brave chick, Chickadee, who had paid the highest price. Now, she and her kin, who Cordelia had saved in the flood were now gone, all at the paws of the vile cat. The brazen attack on Cordelia and Barry's home nest showed that no nest was safe.

Cordelia looked at her terrified chicks, knowing how close she and Barry had come to losing them. Other mytre flew to see why Corselia had cried out. When they saw the result of the attack on Cordelia's chicks, most swiftly returned to their own nests.

Corxell landed next to Cordelia and asked, "Is everyone alright." Adding, "I chased the cat to the norzela nest, but it's gone now." Everyone was in shock, yet in the middle of their trauma Cordelia was reminded of her promise. *We still haven't named them*, she thought. *How can a mytre with no name go to the Great Flock?* With that she nuzzled Barry with her beak and dropped her head to snuggle under his wing. Then she clicked beaks with her injured mother, Corselia and stroked a wing across the heads of the two small chicks.

"We still haven't named them," Cordelia said softly to Corxell. "I said you would be the first to know and with a cat about I want you to know their names now."

Barry was still breathing hard after his flight and after the trauma of the attack, but he said softly, "I'd like to name them… if it's okay with you, my love?"

Cordelia nodded as Barry took a breath and looked at each chick, then at Corxell and his partner.

"Let's name them for the Valley Clan," Barry suggested, boldly.

"What about 'Vall' for the boy, and 'Valora' for the girl," Barry proposed. Cordelia, Corselia, and Corxell turned their heads to one side as they considered Barry's suggestions.

"Outstanding," Cordelia replied.

"I like them," Corxell declared.

"Wonderful," Cordelia's mother said as she grimaced in pain.

Cordelia was happy that the young were finally named. Now she said, "I will see Vall and Valora soon… and you, of course my love," she added softly, as she embraced her mate.

She looked at her injured mother. "How are your injuries?" she asked.

"Fine," Corselia lied. "I'll be fine, dear," she said cementing the lie.

"Good… because now I have to deal with that cat," Cordelia said with conviction. Now that her chicks had names, Cordelia's countenance shifted. Feelings of anger and rage took hold of her emotions. She had chicks of her own, a partner, a family and the valley clan to consider. This cat had no right to try and destroy her young, her family, her partner, or the valley mytre.

Barry could see the change in her expression. Love and care had been replaced by determination and resolve.

"Barry, my love," she said, "I'll chase that vile cat away for good, you stay and watch the nest."

Without waiting for a reply, she sprang to wing in pursuit of the cat. She hadn't noticed that Corselia was struggling with pain and had slumped to the bottom of the nest.

7

HELP?

Help! I need somebody
Help! Not just anybody
Help! You know I need someone
Help!

The Beatles – 'Help' (1965)

THE CAT WAS not injured in the fight in the nest. Its head hurt a little, but it had sustained no lasting injury and while it ran from the tree and dodged the sweeping mytre that chased it along the driveway, the cat was unharmed and even more driven to destroy the valley mytre and their friends. She ran for a short while along the driveway that led to the norzela nest, then hoping to hide, she turned off after passing the human dwelling and crept around to the back of the norzela nest.

The cat had seen the norzela nest as it had skulked about the valley in Egnaro's dim light, but now, in the light of Elppa's glow, it looked oddly inviting. The cat had been a house cat once and as it approached the norzela nest it recalled the human word for the dwelling - house.

Taking note of the activity at the back of the house, the cat saw the small dog. *In a fight, this hairy mat would be less trouble than a quoll*, she thought. She knew that norzela always come out near the end of Elppa's glow, so she found a warm place to lay hidden from the sleepy dog, where she could watch both the dog, and the back door. *I'll wait here and see who comes along. Maybe they'll take pity on a lost bedraggled cat,* she thought.

-0-

The scouts, Karnny and Waytsill flew far and deep into the upper valley near the escarpment looking to confirm Chickadee's story and to find the bower Cordelia had described. They were not gone long, partly because fear meant they didn't want to stay far from the valley, and partly as they had soon found the evidence they sought. Torn limbs from a host of small mammals and the feathers and bones of many birds and lizard littered the upper valley floor. It was a shocking sight and one the two young mytre had never seen before. The only thing they didn't see was the cat.

Their return triggered another emergency elpitlum, where they gave their report to confirm Cordelia and Chickadee's findings, and embellish the horror of the cat's destruction.

"We need a solution to the cat's arrival," Cordelia suggested.

"But we also need to know where it is hiding and where it might strike next," Waytjulia proposed.

"This is a truly ferocious hunter and killer, and I have never had to deal with one of this level of destruction before," Waytbill offered, sounding concerned.

They were meeting on the lawn beside the creek. Given the news about the horror of the cat, none of the mytre wanted to be on the ground long and every branch that blew in the wind, caused a wave of panic to ripple through the gathered mytre, with many lifting into the sky at any false alarm. It made it almost impossible to discuss anything without their being repeated interruptions. Most mytre had come out of fear, and few wanted to be away from their chicks for too long. And as the discussion progressed, cries and rumblings of, "There's a cat coming", gripped and spooked or paralysed the assembled mytre.

"This is no use," Barry whispered to Cordelia, "look at the panic in their eyes."

45

"We have no plan, no defence," she replied. "If we had a plan we might have hope."

"I have never fought a cat before and I know very few mytre who have… and survived," Waytbill said softly. He was whispering but he'd been overheard by one ex-Krat clan mytre who said, "Lord Kratt drove one off once. He'd have known what to do."

"That was a domestic cat, not a real cat at all, really. Not a wild feral keere monster," another listening mytre put in.

"Anyway, I am not so sure Kratt did drive off the cat. I think it was the fire that really finished it off. Because I'm sure it was here up to the fire, and we never saw it after the fire," one of the ex-Kar clan-mytre proposed. The mood at the elpitlum grew bleak as the conversation stumbled on with no plan in sight and some old animosities bubbling to the surface.

"Does anyone have a plan, or a way to defeat the keere monster?" Barry asked desperately.

"We could all leave, go to the eucalypt forest, like we did before, Waytjulia suggested meekly. There was a murmur of disapproval, before Barry said, "Any other ideas?"

No one spoke.

Then one of the former Krat clan members spoke of the reality of their situation saying, "While we are all Valley Clan here, in our nests we are simply family groups. If the cat comes it will be to fight with only one or two mytre at a time, if only we could fight it as the whole Valley Clan. As we stand, the cat will divide and conquer, going from nest tree to nest tree at night, in the cover of Egnaro's shadows. How can the Valley Clan overcome such keere? Lord Kratt would have known," he concluded.

"But Lord Kratt is gone," Waytbill replied, tersely, "and we don't know what he'd have done even if he'd survived, given that he hadn't faced a true wild cat."

Cordelia spoke quietly, "I might have a plan," she said slowly as it formed in her mind. "While we can fly sorties over the valley during the day, why don't we gather all the scouts and single mytre without chicks in the large gum tree at the centre of the valley lands and sky. Then at night they can respond to any call for help from a family group in any part of the valley, with only a short flight to come to their aid."

"A sort of… flying squad…" Karnny added, slowly.

"Yes, a rapid response flying squad," Cordelia clarified.

"It's something," Waytbill agreed with a tired voice. Adding, "It might work, but it's reactive, rather than proactive. It means we can only come to the aid of one of the nests after one or other of the Valley Clan nest trees is under attack."

"But it will buy us more time," Barry said hopefully, suddenly keen and full spirited in support of the idea.

"More time for what?" Waytbill asked, concerned.

"For a more permanent solution," Cordelia said, resigned to the incomplete nature of her plan. She was worried about something the former Krat clan mytre said, about how vulnerable they were as family groups and Cordelia knew her suggestion wasn't the real answer to the crisis they faced.

"We can keep our scout patrols up all through Elppa's passage to search for the cat and rotate the mytre in each flight. At least then we might get some warning of the cat's movements and location," Cordelia concluded.

Like Cordelia, Waytbill knew this was only half a plan, and he knew the cat was most likely to come, as the other mytre had suggested, with Egnaro's dark. Although, as he had no solution either he could think of nothing more to add. They all reluctantly agreed to Cordelia's suggestion, and although the members of the Valley Clan saw they had some sort of action planned, it failed to lift their hope, and many flew back to their nests still fearful and still unsure.

-0-

Cordelia held Barry back as most of the others took off. "I want to come back to the nest, but I need to look about once more and try and find the cat's resting place," she explained. Adding, "You go back to the nest and take care of the chicks and Corselia, I fear she is more badly injured than she is letting on."

Barry knew that arguing was no use and while he hated the idea of her flying alone, he nodded and watched as she lifted into the air.

"Where is Cordelia going?" Karnny asked, with concern.

Barry looked resigned to her taking risks and said, with trepidation in his voice, "She has flown off to find the cat."

Karnny looked at him, shocked. "Alone?" he gasped.

"She is worried that our nest and chicks are very close to the norzela nest, where we last saw the cat, and she wants to explore there once more." Barry knew the search had risks, but he also knew she was not afraid to help protect the valley or her chicks.

Karnny looked concerned. "She told us never to fly alone, but she constantly takes off to search and explore by herself," he protested. "I hope she'll be safe."

"I'd better get back to the chicks," Barry said, as he prepared for flight, "She'll be alright, I hope, she is brave but not foolish."

"Maybe I should go and join her?" Karnny offered.

As he finished speaking, a far-off screech made them both crouch as if ready to fly, but they soon realised it was too far away to be an immediate attack on them. Then Barry and Karnny had the same thought, *Did that come from the norzela nest... was that, Cordelia.*

-0-

Cordelia flew quickly to the norzela nest, searching as she flew for the hiding cat. She looped around the house and saw Jock asleep near his kennel. *He might have seen the keere beast,* she thought. Cordelia swooped in quickly and landed on the lawn, before striding briskly over toward Jock.

Jock opened his eyes and said sleepily, "I'm too tired to play now."

"Jock, mate," Cordelia cried, insistently, "wake up, have you seen the ginger cat?" Jock stretched and stood before walking a few steps toward Cordelia with his tail wagging. He thought this must be one of Cordelia's games and he was about to reply, when he saw the cat rise from under one of the native Australian mint bushes (Prostanthera ovalifolia) behind Cordelia and rush at her.

"Look out..." Jock shouted. But it was too late. The cat was stealthy and swift and within a wing's beat, she was on top of Cordelia. Cordelia let out a high-pitched cry as she was struck. But she was unable to lift off and within an instant she had been flipped over onto her back. The cat pinned her down with its fore paws and sunk her teeth into Cordelia's wing at the shoulder. She cried out in pain again and tried desperately to kick out at her attacker with her claws. Jock ran up to the fight and barked loudly as he bounced around without making any attempt to intervene.

"I have you now, bird," the cat said menacingly. Cordelia tried to flap her wings and get away, but the one that had been bitten, the same one she'd injured on the trip to the station, would not respond and all Cordelia could do was wince in pain.

"First I will kill you, then all your kin, bird," the cat rasped in her ear as she crouched low over her captured prey.

"Maybe, cat," Cordelia whispered through a tight beak. "But before I die you need to know that I am Cordelia the brave, friend of Gary the wedge tail eagle, only son of Garth, grandson of Graham, great grandson of George, and descendant of the Great Gus from the western mountain cliffs. I am also the partner of Barry of the Bar clan and faithful member of the Valley Clan. It will take more than a vile cat like you to send me to the Great Flock of Elppa."

"And yet I have you under my claws... bird," the cat replied with a snarl. Jock continued to bark as he bounced and padded around the fighting pair.

Suddenly, the back door opened, and Tran came out to see what all the fuss was.

"Jock…" Tran cried, "get away from them," he added as he strode over to the cat and bird on his back lawn.

"Cat, what are you doing, get away from that bird, go on… stop it!" The cat was reluctant to leave her captive. She made to bite into Cordelia's neck, but Tran was swift, and he snatched the crouching cat up from the bird and held it at arms-length before calling out, to his wife, Val.

"Val, bring me a cardboard box, luv. I think this bird is injured." He placed the cat down on the lawn and stood between the cat and the bird as he scooped Cordelia into his hand. Cordelia tried in vain to fly and began to peck at Tran's hand as he held her tightly, but her energy was spent, and her blows were weak and ineffective.

"Here, put the bird in here," Val said as she stepped across the lawn with a cardboard box. Within a moment Cordelia was inside the dark confines of the box. She tried to flap but this brought on spasms of pain, and she resigned herself to sitting still and awaiting her fate. *At least,* she thought, *the vile cat is not about to kill me.*

8

THE CAT FINDS A NEW HOME

Now, Old Mister Johnson had troubles of his own
He had a yellow cat who wouldn't leave his home;
He tried and he tried to give the cat away
He gave it to a man goin' far, far away

But the cat came back the very next day
The cat came back, they thought he was a goner
But the cat came back; he just couldn't stay away
Give me a "Meow", go

Harry S. Miller – 'The Cat Came Back' (1894)

BARRY FLEW AS FAST as he could to the home tree, accompanied by Karnny. They landed and Barry asked Corselia, "Is Cordelia here?" Corselia lay in the nest with the two small chicks, Vall and Valora at her side. They both saw how pale she looked and how listless she seemed.

"No… why, what's the matter?" she muttered, still disorientated.

Barry looked at the small chicks, "Stay here with Corselia," he demanded, adding, "Karnny, stay here to watch over them please."

"Where else could we go?" Vall, the male chick replied sounding confused and scared. Barry smiled reassuringly at his chick and flashed a look of determination to Corselia and Karnny before hopping off the nest's lip and flying rapidly towards the norzela nest.

Worry or concern about the vile cat had left him, now all he wanted to do was find Cordelia.

"Cordelia...Cordelia," he called as he ducked and dived between the branches of the trees on the side of the driveway that led to the norzela's nest. As he flew, he saw a white car rising a cloud of dust as it drove along the unsealed driveway. It stopped briefly at the sealed road before turning right and disappearing. He thought little of it, and he refocused on the search for his partner.

Barry flew twice around the norzela nest, once over the dam, and because he also knew of the dog, he landed on the lawn at the back of the norzela nest to ask it some questions.

Jock was laying in his kennel, and he sat up as soon as he saw Barry. They had never met before, but Barry thought Jock seemed sad and shy, and as Barry approached, Jock didn't wag his tail or rush to greet the new mytre. Instead, Jock simply sat up and hung his head. Barry started to approach the small dog. He'd never had much to do with them, like Cordelia had, and he approached cautiously.

Then Barry saw the cat. It was looking at him, as it sat preening its ears from a window-ledge, inside the norzela nest. The cat seemed to be smirking and as it looked at Barry it had a sort of self-satisfied grin. Then it slashed a paw full of claws across the glass, as if to strike out at Barry. Barry gave an involuntary hop into the air, but he knew, for now at least, the cat was unable to harm him. Recognising he was safe, he hop-stepped over to Jock and asked, "Have you seen Cordelia? I'm Barry, her partner."

Jock's tail immediately fell flat, his ears drooped, and his eyes began to swell with tears.

"Gone... taken," was all he could say in a soft bark.

Barry was shocked, "What do you mean?" he demanded half knowing what Jock would say.

"Killed, dead, taken away," he said through a flood of tears. "The cat did it," Jock offered, barking at the ginger cat now sitting comfortably on the window ledge as it continued to preen and pamper itself in the comfort of the norzela nest. "Then my norzela master put her body in a box," Jock concluded.

"Dead…" Barry said softly, "No…?"

"Look," said Jock, pointing at the evidence of a tussle on the lawn. Cat fur and a few long black feathers lay on the lawn around him.

"No… it can't be…" Barry said in disbelief.

"Strong cat," Jock said, "cruel cat," he added sadly. "No more games," he lamented softly as he stepped back into his kennel shaking his shaggy head. Barry was left with the evidence of the cat's victory.

The cat exposed the claws on one of its paws and drew them down the glass making a piercing scratching sound, getting Barry's attention. Barry looked up at the window, before the cat drew their claws slowly across her own throat.

"You're next," the cat hissed, before suddenly, it was snatched up by a young teenage girl and cuddled to her chest.

"I'm going to call you… Meggie," she said as she clutched the cat tightly. The cat went limp as it instantly shed the cloak of a hunter and once more became the gentle, ginger pussy cat. Barry could see it was an act, but with Cordelia gone, his grief overwhelmed him, and he struggled to see how the Valley Clan could be ready for when the cat came out from the norzela nest and into their valley.

Barry's head spun. Cordelia was gone. *How would they all cope? How will I cope without her*, he thought as he sank deeper into despondency. As if in a daze, he thanked Jock before rising slowly into the air, his actions almost robotic. His heart was heavy with loss, and he struggled to find height as he flew, knowing the burden of bad news he carried back to his nest tree, and the Valley Clan.

-0-

Barry flew back to the nest tree in the ghost gum. It was only a short distance from the norzela nest, but he was out of breath and practically beside himself as he landed. Corselia and Karnny could see he was distressed.

"What's the matter Barry?" she asked, through her own pain. He told her what he knew, about what Jock has said of Cordelia's end, about the cat being inside the norzela nest and about the evidence he'd found on the lawn. Corselia could hardly believe what he was saying, and it took a while before Barry could make her believe what he had heard.

"Cordelia is gone, dead, killed by the cat," he repeated as he carefully hugged Cordelia's mother.

"What?... No..." Karnny cried, in disbelief. Karnny wanted to see for himself, and he took off toward the norzela nest, calling back, "I'll find her. She can't be gone."

-0-

Word soon spread and mytre from across the valley flew to the nest tree to hear the news for themselves. Barry found it became more real with each retelling of the disaster. Waytbill and Waytjulia were devastated and Corxell struggled to comprehend the news, becoming angry to the point where he could no longer hear the dreadful news over and over. He flew away to the central nest tree to be with his thoughts. There he became almost inconsolable as he cried for the loss of his sister.

"What will we do now?" Many of the mytre asked fearful for their own welfare and the future of the Valley Clan. Many offered their condolences to Barry and Corselia and all wished Cordelia a safe and speedy transition to the Great Flock of Elppa.

Karney returned from the norzela nest. He's seen the cat through a window and the feathers on the lawn, but still he refused to believe it.

"She can't be dead," he cried, "she has the gift of foresight, she is a swift and cunning mytre, how could an evil and spiteful cat catch and kill her? And where is her body?" he demanded to know.

"The norzela took it," Barry said through sobs and tears. "It was what Jock the dog told me. Jock saw her killed and then he saw the norzela put her body in a box."

"But what did they do with her body?" Karnny persisted.

"They took it… I told you, she is gone, the fight on the lawn was real, you saw the feathers, I saw the cat snarl and gloat." Barry took a breath. "Now stop this," Barry demanded, becoming frustrated with Karnny. "Now, leave us to our grief," Barry snapped.

"The cat will soon return," Waytjulia suggested fearfully. "Without Cordelia's foresight we are blind and now the cat will be emboldened and come to take our chicks." A ripple of dread ran through the mytre gathered at the nest tree.

"She will come at night," Barry said, "we must have our rapid response team ready as soon as Egnaro has set."

"I will lead them," Karney suggested, feeling unable to do anything else, "All you have to do is call and we will come to your aid." None of the birds looked certain their rapid response squad plan would work and without Cordelia to give them hope or bolster their courage all their hearts sank. Then with the gradual fall of Elppa, the Valley Clan faced the impending darkness with growing trepidation.

9

A GREAT LOSS

All the way, all the way
I miss your touch baby, yeah
Like a thief in the night
It can't be right...
(Like a thief)
I know where your place is
And it's not with him

Rolling Stones – 'Thief in the Night' (1997)

NO MYTRE SLEPT throughout the whole passage of Egnaro. All through Egnaro's dim glow the parents and partners of each nest tree stayed awake and vigilant. The rapid response team of Karnny, Waytsill and Corxill sat eager and alert in case there were screeches or sounds that the cat was on the prowl.

There were three false calls when over cautious mytre sounded the alarm, usually when other creatures wandered across the valley in the night. Firstly, the three young mytre where called out for a passing brown rat. This small rodent was enough to send the mytres gathered in their nests near the norzela park into near panic. Later in the darkness, twice, the flying squad were called out when a wombat came up from the eucalypt forest in search of fruit from the remnants of the orchard.

The mytre were all exhausted. From the lack of sleep and from the emotional strain of an anticipated attack and fear.

None of the valley mytre knew but Tran had forbidden the new ginger cat to be allowed out of their house. Their daughter was delighted and cuddled or tried to play with the cat long into the evening. But she became annoyed when the cat seemed unresponsive to enticements to play. Even scratching her on the hand at one point. After that the cat was ignored.

"This doesn't seem like a lost domestic cat," Tran said after bandaging his daughter's hand. "It seems to me that it could be a feral cat that has decided to stay near our house. In the hope of a free meal or a warm place to sleep," he speculated.

"We can keep it in tonight, there is a sand tray ready near the back door," Val said, "but it will have to be let out at some point, we can't keep it in all the time."

"I'll put the collar and bell on tomorrow then it should be safe to be let out," Tran offered, "It'll be interesting to see if it comes back."

Worn down by the cat's lack of charm, Tran's daughter said, defiantly, "Well I don't want it in my room tonight. Leave it in the laundry, by the back door." The cat didn't seem to mind and after enjoying a meal of tinned meat and fresh milk, it settled into a warm blanket to sleep in the laundry, near the norzela's back door.

-0-

Barry was still struggling to process the news of Cordelia's death, and like the other valley mytre had not slept at all. Corselia was feeling better physically, although the shock of Cordelia's passing had left her feeling both despondent and lost. She was still struggling to move, let alone fly and she was no help with feeding Vall and Valora. Barry had started to search for food, and he returned to the nest with a few morsels for the young and even some for Corselia. But his heart wasn't in the search, and he could think of nothing else but Cordelia. Barry fed the chicks and dropped a beak full of food, for Corselia.

"You have to leave the nest tree," Corselia suggested as she snatched up the small grub and swallowed it. "It's not safe here and you are too close to the cat if it's now living in the norzela nest."

"I know," Barry agreed, "The chicks will have to fledge during the course of Elppa's passage, so we can move to a new nest, before Egnaro's return… but they are still small…" He paused, before asking, "How well are you? Can you fly? You still look injured, and I cannot leave you here alone even if the chicks can move."

"I'll be fine to fly before Egnaro," she reassured him.

Barry was not convinced, but he pressed on, gathering the two chicks under his wings and explaining what he planned to do. "There are old nests in the Norfolk Island Pines on the east of the valley and before Egnaro's return you will need to fly with Corselia and I to find a new home."

All birds fear fledging. It is a true and genuine leap into the unknown and not all birds survive their first flight. "Stay here now," Barry said, "I will find some more food to help build your strength before you fly, then I'll help you find your wings."

Once the chicks were fed, Barry encouraged first Vall and then Valora to the lip of the nest. "Vall you will fly first," he instructed. A breeze had risen as nwod passed and it offered a slight updraft making flight easier. But still Vall felt nervous as he looked into the void below him.

"Get ready, Vall," Barry instructed, "glide, then try to catch the air as you near the ground. I'll fly with you, but don't look at me, focus on your own wings and feel the air catch in your feathers as you glide… then once you have the wind, flap your wings and fly… ready son?" he asked finally.

"Ready father," Vall replied. *I wish Cordelia were here*, he thought, *she would be so much better at this than I am*. Barry counted, "One, two, three, fly." Then they both leapt from the nest in unison.

Their flight was short but spectacular. Vall looked every bit as if he had flown before and was quickly rising and gliding, diving and skipping on the breeze. Landing was another matter and like most mytre chicks he struggled with his landing as he tried to follow Barry back to a branch near the nest.

"Again," Barry said, before dropping from the branch to lead Vall in a second flight. They practiced all through Elppa's passing, with Valora joining Barry for her instruction before all three mytre struck out from the branch repeatedly, quickly gaining skill and honing their gift for flight. Before Egnaro's return, the two chicks were accomplished in the basics of flight and Barry felt sure they'd be able to reach a new nest in the pine trees by the norzela park. But Corselia had not taken part and as Elppa's light dimmed he began to worry that her ability or strength to fly had not returned as they had hoped.

"Can you fly?" Barry asked in a whisper, as the chicks chattered excitedly.

"I fear not, Barry," Corselia replied almost exhausted with the effort of talking.

"It's not just that my wounds are not healing, but I fear the loss of Cordelia has broken my heart, my spirit. I don't want to go on."

"But if you stay here and the cat returns, how will we protect you?" Barry asked still in a low voice.

"That will be in Elppa's rays I am afraid, my boy," she said resigned to her fate. She looked at Barry with sad eyes, and added softly, "Look after the young. Teach them about their mother and help make the Valley Clan strong. Now fly... before Egnaro makes the journey too difficult."

Barry touched her beak with his and said gently, "Elppa's blessing on you." Then he turned, hopped up on to the lip of the nest, and called the chicks over to his side. Corselia watched them go and made herself comfortable in the nest.

-0-

The flight across to the pine trees took only a short while and Barry and the chicks were soon ensconced in the nest Corselia had defended when Silas and the lizard had attacked. It was high and it was strong, but it felt strange being away from their home tree.

Karnny, Waytsill and Corxell, although exhausted, began to prepare for their Egnaro vigil over the valley. To start with, each bird flew around to all the nest trees checking with the clan members and reminding the mytre what to do if they were attacked. It was by chance that Corxell flew to his old nest tree and found his mother resting alone.

"Mother?" he asked, sounding confused.

"I'm okay, just too tired to fly," she reassured him, lying.

"You can't stay here, what if the cat were to come again?" Corxell demanded.

"I'll call you… don't worry," Corselia reassured him, lying again. She felt weak and doubted she would have the strength to call out for help, let alone fight off the cat. But she was unafraid, having lost her first son to the eagle, her partner to the norzela car, her daughter to the cat and her ability to fly, because of a broken heart. A calmness overcame her, and she felt that Elppa had abandoned her and that in his loss she had nothing else to worry about. Suddenly, staying alone in the nest was an easy thing to accept, and she thought, *Should the cat come, I can make it pay for my daughter's life.*

"I'll stay with you tonight," her only surviving son said. "Do you remember when we fled the valley when Lord Kratt took over at the elpitlum? Well, you watched over me on our flight, and now… I'll watch over you and make sure no harm comes to you, mother." He was sobbing as he spoke but found a new resolve that grew from his love for his mother.

"No…" she said softly, adding, "go to Barry and the chicks in the pine tree. Help protect the chicks… they might need you more." Corxell could see she was tired and wanted nothing more than to rest in the comfort of the nest.

"You rest mother," he said, softly through a sob. He flew to a branch just beyond the nest and perched there, so that he could keep watch over his mother, out of sight as she slept.

-0-

Barry knew that the valley mytre were tired and stretched when it came to keeping a watch on the cat. So, he flew over to Karney and Waytsill at the flying squad tree shortly before Egnaro's appearance.

"I have an idea," Barry suggested. "Karnny, will you watch my chicks while I go and talk to the dog, Jock."

"Why?" they asked stunned at the suggestion.

"I want to ask him to help us watch the cat."

"Will he do it?" Karnny asked.

Waytsill asked, "Can we trust him?"

"I don't know, but it's a risk I'm willing to take to help make the valley safe," Barry replied.

Karnny agreed and flew away to Barry's new nest, while Barry flew quickly back across the valley and landed on the lawn near Jock's kennel. He quickly scanned the area for the cat. He saw it sitting back in the window ledge inside the norzela nest and knew again that at least for the moment he was safe. Quickly he called out to Jock, "Jock, are you there?" Jock was asleep and yawned before responding.

"What do you want? It's nearly supper time, isn't it?" Jock barked.

Barry didn't know but he persisted, "Jock, can I ask you for a favour?"

The small dog yawned again and thought about chasing the irritating bird away, but couldn't be bothered so he said, "What do you want, bird?"

"I need a spy..." Barry explained cryptically, "a clever spy."

"A spy?" Jock mused. "To do what?" Jock asked, as he warmed to the idea.

"I… well the birds of the valley, want you to keep an eye out for the terrible cat who seems to be living here now."

"To spy on it you mean?"

"Yes, and to warn us if you see it leave the norzela nest," Barry clarified.

"How?" Jock barked.

"Just watch the house, then if it comes outside, bark as loudly as you can, to tell us that it is on the loose… simple really."

"What do I get in return for being your spy?" Jock asked.

Barry thought for a moment, then said, "Our appreciation for one thing. The friendship and kindness of all the valley mytre and the title of best dog of the valley."

"Oh, wonderful," Jock snapped, instantly barking, "I'll do it."

Barry could see that Elppa had almost gone and that Egnaro was only a short flight away, so he called out, "Thank you," to Jock and flapped into the gloomy sky.

The cat sitting on the window ledge had been witness to the bird and the dog's conversation and although she couldn't hear any of it, she was sure that the dog, Jock, and the mytre were trying to develop a plan. *And this just wouldn't do*, she thought.

-0-

The evening was well underway when the cat was let out. Tran had made sure that before it had been allowed to go outside, he'd placed the collar and bell about its neck. The cat hated it and immediately tried to squeeze out of the collar. It felt uncomfortable and unfamiliar about its neck. But worse… it made a tell-tail ring with almost every step. No matter how much the cat squirmed and tried to snag the collar she was unable to remove it.

The cat remembered when it had worn a bell before, and she also remembered how difficult hunting had been with the ringing forever giving her location and movement away. But for now, she thought, *I'll have to make do as well as I can, until I can find a way out of the noose.*

Jock saw the cat come from the back door and immediately started to bark at the top of his lungs. In the valley, cries rang from nest tree to nest tree, 'The cat is loose, be aware.' Barry's plan had worked.

The cat padded over to Jock's kennel silently and stood at the opening to the kennel, bell jingling brightly. Immediately, Jock stopped barking and moved to the back of his kennel to cower. He had seen the fight with Cordelia and knew how vicious the cat could be. *Maybe she'll just leave me alone*, Jock thought. He was soon disappointed as the cat said, "Stay out of my way, or you'll end up like the stupid bird."

Jock barked back bravely, "This is my kennel, you can't come in and anyway I'm not afraid of you." His courage was only a ruse, and it left him as soon as the cat stepped further into the opening of the kennel. Jock moved slowly back into the dark recesses of his wooden home.

"If I were you, dog," the cat snarled, "I'd stay well away from me, and those birds, or you might find yourself in a whole lot of trouble."

"What trouble?" Jock snapped back, finding courage he never thought he had. With that, the cat slashed out with a paw, claws out. Jock drew back quickly, but not quickly enough, and a set of deep scratches appeared across his face.

"That kind for one," the cat announced boldly. Then she raised her paw to strike again. "Now, no more barking or you'll pay," the cat ordered.

Jock cowered at the back of the kennel and braced for the second slash, but it didn't come, and he let out a sigh of relief as he heard the jingle of bells slowly fading off into the distance.

-0-

For the second night in a row, the rapid respond squad were being called to suspicious but false reports of there being a cat in the valley. Again, a wombat spooked members of the Valley Clan living near the eucalypt forest. A number of false reports were made because even the arrival of the flying squad spooked various nervous mytre who, because of their hyper fear, thought somehow the cat could now fly.

Karnny and Waytsill were especially worn out because Corxell had not come back to join them in the central tree and had instead stayed near his mother to watch over her in the ghost gum nest tree. Few mytre had rested and while most sang the Elppa chorus, it sounded dull and lacklustre as the mytre struggled with their nerves, fear and exhaustion.

For the second night in a row there was no sign of the cat in the valley. None of the valley mytre knew about the bell around the cat's neck and many assumed it was now locked in the norzela nest and would not trouble them again. Barry and the mytre of the rapid response squad suspected there may be another reason for the cat's 'no show', because they all knew it had been released from the norzela nest. Jock's barked warning had worked well, and Barry made a mental note to fly over to thank Jock before Elppa's passing.

None of the mytre knew that, while none of the valley mytre were injured, the cat had still managed to harm them. Because, while the cat had been watching Jock and Barry talk at the previous passing of Elppa, she had concocted a plan to eliminate the Valley Clan's ally, Jock, and kill their early warning system. It was this plan that the cat had been employed in while Egnaro ruled the sky.

The plan had four parts. The first involved finding a weak spot in the chicken coop and getting inside. The bell at her neck hindered her considerably but the cat reasoned that for all the trouble it would cause, leaving it on might be to her advantage. The chicken coop was made with wire and wood with six hinged hatches for collecting the eggs without going into the coop. She could see no weak spots low to the ground.

The cat sniffed around at all the doors and hatches, but they seemed to be only one weak place for her to squeeze into the coop and while this hatch looked loose, it appeared she couldn't get in that way. But she found that on top of the coop, part of the wire had not been bound together well and a small gap existed were two sheets of wire over lapped. This left a gap, that was almost exactly cat sized.

Silently the cat dropped into the coop. The second part of her plan involved making sure she could escape back the way she had come or find a new way to escape. This had proved more difficult. The top of the coop was reachable, but the cat knew it would be impossible to squeeze back out through the wire and hold onto the high wire at the same time. The way in would be no use as an escape.

The cat moved slowly and every time she moved to search for a new exit, her bell chimed and resulted in a mild murmur from the assembled hens. Therefore, the cat needed to move slowly and stealthily through the coop hoping to leave the chickens rested and quiet...at least for now. Then she saw a way out. One of the hatches, that allowed the norzela to reach into the coop and collect eggs, the loose one she'd seen before, was left undone.

This meant the cat could see that by pushing on the hatch, it would swing up and open allowing her to get out quickly. She chastised herself silently for not seeing this fault on her inspection of the external hatch doors, but she knew she had been doubly lucky as the broken hatch latch was one that had no chicken roosting in front of it, and it was only the lack of a resident chicken that allowed her to see the chink of Egnaro's light that signalled that the hatch was a little ajar.

So, she was in, and she had a way out. Part three of her plan meant she would have to repeat the process by getting out and then back in before the final stage of her plan could be employed. Part three was simple. The cat gathered a mouth full of chicken feathers and left the coop through the hatch.

She was back in a short while, without the feathers and she waited quietly outside the coop making sure everything near the norzela nest was still and that there were no birds waiting to upset her plans.

All was quiet. Even Jock hadn't stirred when she had climbed onto the top of his kennel and dropped her mouth full of chicken feathers down into its opening. As she waited, she thought, *He'll get the blame, I'm sure.* She couldn't help grinning widely at her own cunning and wit.

Egnaro had almost passed by the final part of her passage. The orb was still full but not far from touching the western horizon. *Time to act*, she thought as she started the fourth part of her plan. Again, she moved slowly and climbed back up to the loosened wire on the top of the coop. She dropped onto the soil on the chicken coop floor, and her bells briefly jangled before the cat snatched at them to hold them silent. She looked to see if her escape hatch was still vacant, then as stealthily as she could, she set about the chicken's murder.

The cat would normally attack in a frenzy of violence, but she acted as quietly and as skilfully as she could, first taking the rooster by the throat and choking him. Then she moved from chicken-to-chicken dispatching each like a ninja cat, silent and deadly. A few chickens woke to the danger, but the cat was on them before they could make too much noise. Jock heard the noise from the coop at one point, but put it down to the approach of Elppa, and went back to sleep.

Before dawn, all twelve chickens had been killed. Now silent the cat began to tear the chickens apart in a silent frensy to make it look like a shocking vicious mass murder by an unhinged and vengeful animal... a fox, or a dog perhaps. Just as Elppa rose over the eastern valley hills the cat moved away to the native Australian mint bush by the lawn and began to preen herself, cleaning away any evidence that she could have been responsible for the chicken attack. Then she drifted off to sleep. It had been a long night.

10

JOCK'S CHAIN

Listen to the wind blow
Watch the sun rise
Run in the shadows
Damn your love, damn your lies
And if you don't love me now
You will never love me again

I can still hear you sayin'

You would never break the chain

Fleetwood Mac – 'Break the Chain' (1977)

TRAN HAD SLEPT IN. "Are you going to get up or what?" Val asked sounding annoyed.

What happened to that bloody rooster, Tran thought. It was not like him to sleep in, and he usually depended on the rooster's early morning call to wake him. *Clearly something isn't right,* he thought. "I'll be ready soon," Tran called to his wife, and he dressed and made ready to check on the chicken coop.

"Would you like eggs with your bacon, luv? she called out to her husband.

"Yes, I'll bring some back from the hen house once I have checked on the sleepy rooster," he replied as he stepped through the kitchen and out the back door.

He came racing back into the house a few minutes later. "Bloody dog's been an attacked the hens," he said angrily. "You should see the mess he's made of the hen house." Tran added, "Bloody disaster. It looks like not a single chicken has been left alive."

"What?" Val exclaimed doubtfully, "The dog wouldn't do that," she said in Jock's defence.

"Well, there are dead chickens in the coop and chicken feathers in its bloody kennel, and I'm sure they didn't just fly there on their own." He was in the process of grabbing a metal chain and lead from a hook in the laundry.

"I'll deal properly with that dog later but for now he'll have to stay chained to his kennel."

Val hadn't seen Tran this cross in a long time. She washed her hands under the tap before going outside to look at the destruction and the evidence herself. She could see that the hens and the rooster had been savagely killed, and she could see the few feathers in the opening of the kennel, but something didn't feel right. Jock had never so much as shown any interest in the chickens, even when they were loose in the yard.

"Why didn't we hear the attack, in the night," she asked Tran as he came back outside. "Why didn't we wake up. Surely an attack like this by a dog would have caused a whole lot of noise. But we didn't hear a thing, did we?"

Tran stopped to consider her suggestion. "It could have been a fox," he pondered, but he'd not seen or heard of any foxes in the area. He thought, *And I'd surely have heard a fox attack too.*

"Could it have been the cat?" Val offered.

"I doubt it," Tran said as he checked the chain's latch. "The cat was wearing the bell and surely that would have alerted the chickens or at least made them squark and cluck." He paused, as he pondered the matter further, "And if it wasn't the dog, how else would the feathers have turned up in his kennel?"

"Sup'ose," Val conceded, "But I never felt the dog was a killer, and remember, the cat was outside last night."

Tran clipped the end of the chain with a clasp onto Jock's collar and hooked the other end over a nail protruding from his kennel.

"No food for you today," Tran said as he stepped back into the house.

"Why don't we call the vet to come out, and see if they can tell us what might have happened?

"And how we can go about cleaning up this mess," Tran added agreeing with the suggestion. "Bloody dog," he muttered to himself, as he paced over to the back door and into the house.

-0-

The cat, her belly full, lay under the pink-purple flowers of the native mint bush (Prostanthera ovalifolia) by the front driveway, sleeping on after her busy night. She could see the look of confusion on Jock's face and saw the chain holding him captive to the kennel. *He'll not help those bothersome birds again*, she thought.

-0-

After lunch, the vet came to see Tran and Val, and to look at the mess in the chicken coop.

"It's a good job I've eaten," she said as she looked at the carnage in the hen house. "This would've been enough to put me off my lunch if I'd come earlier," she added.

"Did the dog do this?" Tran asked.

"That dog?" the vet asked pointing at the dog chained to the kennel. "I very much doubt it," she said, "I can concede that it's small enough to get into the coop, but I suspect the culprit is more agile by far." She reached up onto the wire at the top of the coop and pulled down a few tuffs of hair.

"Looks like a feral cat or maybe a fox has been at them," she concluded handing a few strands of ginger hair over to Tran to examine. "As well," she added, gesturing to the hen carcases, "a dog would likely have eaten more of the hens not just torn them to bits like this."

"I said it might have been that cat," Val declared triumphantly. Adding as she looked around the garden, "I wonder where it's gone?"

"But how did the feathers get into the kennel?" Tran questioned aloud.

"Could they have been blown there?" the vet suggested meekly.

"Or placed there?" Val said, quizzically.

"A bloody mystery," Tran concluded. "But a bloody disaster for our hens too."

"You might be best digging a pit and burning the carcases in it. To stop other animals coming to dig them up," the vet said, "I'd wait a while to restock and fix the few weak spots in the coop's construction too." The vet walked over to Jock.

"Nice little dog this, but not a chicken killer. Not this sweety," she said patting the dog behind the ears. Then standing she said, "Oh...I'll bring that injured magpie back tomorrow, if that's alright? They're territorial, so I'll need to let it go near where you found it," the vet suggested.

"Right-oh," Tran said, "thanks for your help with the injured bird and the chicken problem. I don't sup'ose you know how to catch a feral cat do you?"

-0-

The cat stayed under the mint bush and out of sight all day. She had no intention of returning to the norzela nest and her next task was to find a way to be rid of the collar and bell. A thought had come to her about how to remove it, but she knew she'd need to wait until Egnaro's return before trying her idea.

Jock lay chained to the kennel for the remainder of the day. Tran had left him on the chain while he had dug a shallow pit, and while he and Val had cleaned out the chicken carcasses and hosed down the hen house before setting fire to the pit. Jock had only been able to walk out as far as the short chain would allow, and he spent a most miserable day confined and hungry. He barked and pulled at his collar and chain, and he couldn't understand the abuse he received when he showed his displeasure. *They haven't done this to me before*, he thought. *What was their reason for such disrespectful behaviour*? He had no clue and after getting no one to come to feed him, or take off the chain, or pay him any attention apart from the norzela stranger, he had no choice other than to settle back into the kennel and hope there would be an evening meal coming.

-0-

Egnaro rose over the valley before the cat crept out from under the mint bush. She stretched and clawed at the soil. Then walked silently over to the empty hen house. It still smelt of death, in spite of the norzela's attempt to clean it. The cat jumped up to the top of the chicken coop and sought out the wire where she had squeezed into the coop.

There, the cat tried to catch the clasp of the collar on the wire of the cage. She took great care and worked slowly so as not to make the bell ring out over the garden. The wire was stiff and suitable for her aims but getting it to catch under the collar clasp took repeated attempts and great patience.

Egnaro had risen only a little higher before the collar and the tell-tail bell dropped into the now empty chicken coop. *Finally free*, the cat thought. *Now I'll show those birds of the valley what a skilled hunter can do when angry*. The bell had fallen silently, but as it hit the soil of the coop it jingled a little as it landed. This was enough to alert Jock, and he sprang up, ears erect. *The cat is about*, he thought, and despite his fear, and the cat's warning to stay silent, he began to bark as loudly as he could.

-0-

71

Corselia had remained in the old ghost gum nest watched over by Corxell. Her wounds were recovering, but her heart was broken and her will to live had been extinguished.

"Just leave me," Corselia begged Corxell, "go… be with the other mytre at the flying squad tree. Help defend the Valley Clan. I'll be fine, comfortable, and safe here, I'm sure."

"No… mother," Corxell said, determined to remain with her until she was recovered, or died from her wounds. Nothing she said could move her son from the branch above the nest. Corxell had stayed with his mother throughout the passage of Egnaro when the chicken murders occurred, and throughout the reappearance and passage of Elppa.

From his branch high in the tree, he had seen the arrival and departure of the vet at the norzela nest and smelt the smoke from the fire as the chicken carcasses where burnt. *Death*, he thought, *more death at the hands and claws of the vile cat, I suppose.* He watched over Corselia as she slept, she was breathing only shallow breaths and she hardly moved, apart from spasms of pain. He wished he could entice her to fly, but he could see now that she was spent and broken. During Elppa's passing Corxell had flown to bring her grubs and worms, but she had eaten only a small portion of his offerings. Barry had visited them once to report on the situation in the valley.

"Every mytre is past exhaustion," he said, clearly tired himself. "The flying squad have had no rest and every mother with chicks is on the brink of panic and nervous breakdown. Many want to leave the valley, and it has taken all Waytbill and I could say to keep them on their nests."

"Karnny is tired, although more than any other mytre he seems to have an almost inexhaustible supply of drive. He's been flying to almost every nest with words of encouragement, telling all the Valley Clan mytre that we have survived another Egnaro and that no one else has been taken. Thank goodness for his spirit," Barry added, "I'd have given up myself without his hopeful outlook."

Barry could see Corselia sleeping in the nest. "How is she," he asked, kindly. Corxell lowered his head. "I think she could fly if she had the will to try, but the loss of Cordelia has taken her heart." Corxell could feel his own heart breaking too. But he said softly, "I'll stay here with her in case the cat comes back or in case she finds her courage and spirit again." Barry could see Corxell's fear and sadness, and the tiredness of one who has been emotionally and physically tested.

Barry felt the loss of Cordelia greatly and his heart was crushed by exertion and grief. He had the chicks to consider too. "I need to get back to the chicks, Vall and Valora. They've been very brave, but I can see they don't understand why Cordelia has not returned or why we needed to move to the higher pine tree nest."

Barry added, "I don't mean to pressure you, but with you here, the flying squad is weaker and unable to respond with as much strength should a cat attack come." Corxell knew and could appreciate what Barry was saying.

"But she's my mother…" Corxell replied knowing this was all the defence he'd need. Barry placed a comforting wing on Corxell's shoulder, and said, "Elppa be with you through the following passing of Egnaro." He missed Cordelia and her determination, her optimism and… love.

"Be safe," Barry said, as he lifted into the late Elppa light and flew back to the pine trees near the norzela park.

-0-

As Egnaro rose, the valley was quiet. Darkness grew as a low cloud bank rolled in from the escarpment and cloaked the valley from Egnaro's pale glow. This was the beginning of the third night since Cordelia had been taken. No valley mytre had died under the claws of the cat, although the valley mytre were still on edge, still tired from almost constant vigilance and still unsure what the coming Egnaro would hold.

However, still they waited in anticipation of the attack, most were sure was coming. Some younger mytre spread their view that the cat was gone. That the threat was over and that they could all get some sleep under the cover of Egnaro's cloak. But as the cloud bank rolled through the valley, many of the more experienced and wiser mytre knew the quiet and still were simply the intake of breath before the storm of the cat struck.

Barry's quills stood stiffly as he heard far off in the distance, the low soft barking of a dog. He drew the two chicks closer into his flank and said softly to himself, "It's coming."

11

EGNARO'S CLOAK

Here I am, alone again
Can't get out of this hole I'm in
It's like the walls are closin' in
You can't help me, no one can
I can feel these curtains closin'
I go to open 'em
But something pulls 'em closed again
(*Hello, darkness, my old friend*)

Eminem – 'Darkness' (2020)

THE DARKNESS made the valley feel smaller, tighter and closed in. Instead of the wide spaces between the trees on either side of the creek, the low cloud made the whole valley seem like it was inside a cupboard almost with walls and a ceiling. The escarpment felt closer, and the tops of the trees were covered in mist and cloud. An eery feeling touched many of the valley mytre and it deepened their sense of dread.

The cat moved quickly away from the norzela nest and the yappy dog, across the top of the dam and over to the creek. It's first attack would be on a pair of young mytre who had a nest halfway up a tall gum tree on the eastern side of the creek.

The pair had once been part of the Kar clan. They had survived Lord Kratt, and the fire, the flood, and the lizard attack and made their nest in a tree close to the creek and closer to the escarpment than any of the other mytre nests.

As Egnaro approached, they settled into their nest after their ksud chorus and waited, with growing trepidation as the darkness, the cloud and the chill of Egnaro grew about them.

The cat had seen their nest on an earlier reconnaissance of the valley and knew that the nest held at least one chick. The cat sat at the base of the tree and waited to hear if she had been noticed by the two birds or their chick, before beginning a slow and stealthy climb towards the nest. It took only a short time to ascend the tree, and the cat didn't wait to attack. Instead, she charged at the nest as soon as she had reached the branch it was on.

The two adult mytre had no warning of the cat's approach and were both caught off guard as the cat lunged into the nest. The male mytre was struck first and forced out of the nest. His partner was stunned and paralysed with fear, freezing as the cat slashed and bit, scratched and snarled at her. Within a moment the female mytre lay mortally wounded and unable to react further. Her partner cried out for help and then dived back into the fray pecking and scratching with his beak and claws.

But the cat seemed unharmed as it used its fore paws to swat at the mytre, keeping the distressed bird at paws length. The chick tried to burrow under its mother's body, trying desperately to hide from the claws of its attacker. But his father's attack was too weak, and his mother was unable to do anything to help the little chick.

"Get away from my chick, you vile cat," the male called as he flapped in and out of the air space around the cat, lunging ineffectively with his beak or reaching out with his claws.

The cat, although at first bothered by the bird, felt she had little risk of injury and so focused on finding and killing the chick. It only took a moment. She dragged the chick from under its mother's belly and savagely, viciously bit and mauled the tiny chick with its jaws and teeth.

The chick's father was beyond distress and dived in again and again, trying to hit or claw the vile cat. But his fighting skills were underdeveloped, and he lacked the courage to get too close to the killer to inflict any real damage. Feeling he'd let his family down the male mytre, with nothing left to live for, dived one last time at the cat as it turned to leave the nest. As he did, the cat pivoted and lunged at the diving mytre with an outstretched paw, brisling with claws. The mytre was caught across the beak and face and crashed into a branch as he tried to draw back from the strike.

The cat reacted like lightening, diving onto the mytre's back and forcing the bird hard into the branch, before sinking her teeth into the injured bird's neck. It was over quickly, and the cat, after biting hard into the bird, dropped the lifeless father mytre. He fell dead, to the base of the nest tree.

Karnny and Waytsill of the flying squad, had heard the mytre's call of distress and raced to investigate or help in the fight. Karnny arrived in time to see the male mytre's fall from the tree, and he flew down to the fallen mytre's side. As Karnny landed, the cat came scurrying down the tree trunk and landed with a soft thud about a metre from the two birds.

"The darkness is my friend," she hissed as she crouched low before springing away through the low scrub and into the gloom of Egnaro's domain.

Waytsill landed a moment later and the two young flying squad mytre were stunned to see the destruction of the cat's attack. It was clear that this mytre was dead, and after flying up to the nest they soon found the dead mother mytre with the remains of the mutilated chick at her side. Distraught, and unable to do anything for the three dead mytre, they both flew back to the tall gum tree in the centre of the valley, calling to all the other mytre of the valley as they flew, alerting them that the cat was about, before landing to anxiously await their next distress call.

-0-

The cat stalked through the undergrowth and made her way slowly and silently, like a ginger ninja, through the darkness. The low cloud cloaked her advance into and through the valley, with

Egnaro's light failing to pierce the clouds. The cat's next target was a nest a little way east of the creek and only a short distance from the first tree she had attacked. She was sure all the valley mytre were acutely aware that she was about, and she knew that she would not be able to sneak up on other nests as easily. Still, she moved with care and silently approached her next victims.

The next nest was occupied by two mature mytre. They had been part of the Krat clan and had come with Lord Kratt when he'd led them into the warren during the fire. After Lord Kratt's death they stayed in the valley and stayed loyal to the Valley Clan; even though they always felt anxious about the strength of their new clan. They had followed Lord Kratt and although they had been disappointed with his leadership, he was the only mytre leader they knew, and they stayed loyal even when they felt his leadership was too autocratic. They thought the more open leadership system of the Valley Clan was better, but they still felt like intruders or interlopers when decisions about their future where considered.

This Egnaro, as they settled nervously in their nest, they discussed their future. "At least here in the Valley Clan community decisions are discussed," the female former Krat clan mytre said. "With Lord Kratt we never felt invited to contribute to his clan decisions." They had both supported Kratatora when she had wanted to leave at the height of the lizard invasion, and they were prepared to leave before Cordelia returned with the kookaburra. They were willing to support Kratatora, although, because of their potential mutiny, they felt as if they were still only grudgingly tolerated in their new clan. It was for this reason that they decided not to have chicks this season.

They knew that bringing up chicks required commitment, not just to the chicks, but to the rest, to the wider clan, and it also requires the clan to support the new parents. They were starting to feel at home in the valley, but the lizard invasion and the recent uncertainty with the cat had made them delay their final decision to stay and bring up chicks in their new home.

"It's been three passings of Egnaro and the cat has not attacked," the female former Krat clan mytre said, adding, "we should stay and support the Valley Clan."

"Three days and no attack means only that we are now closer to an attack than three days ago. An attack is inevitable, and I fear imminent," her partner said. The male mytre was sure the valley was cursed. It had been this mytre who had spoken out at the recent elpitlum. "We should leave with Elppa's light," he concluded.

"And where should we go?" his partner asked. 'Where is safe from our mytre enemies?" Here at least we have allies, friends even. This valley is full of compassion, forgiveness, hope, and heart. Kratt brought us none of these things."

"He brought the Kratt clan strength and leadership," her partner protested as he moved to the lip of the nest to pass a dropping.

"But where did it get us? No home, constant worry, murder, death and fighting." She paused, "The valley can be a home for our future young," the female mytre suggested.

"If we can survive the cat. And anyway, the valley seems to have been constant worry, murder, death and fighting, if you ask me," her partner said, bitterly.

The cat could hear them talking high above her, and she used their discussion as a distraction to stealthily approach, up the tree and towards their nest. She had almost reached the nest when the male mytre stepped up onto the lip of the nest to pass a dropping to the base of the tree. It only just missed the cat as she crouched closely to the tree branch she was on. She waited until the bird returned to the nest and then proceeded to climb the short distance to the nest.

When she struck, both birds were snugly next to each other at the bottom of the nest and their discussion seemed to be near its end.

"We can discuss this further, with Elppa's light." The male mytre suggested as he was getting snug next to his partner.

It was at that moment the cat struck.

-0-

"There's another cry for help," Karnny called as he turned his head to get a bearing on the direction. Waytsill agreed saying, "It's to the east, I'll go alone… you stay here in case there is another call for help, and this is a false alarm." With that Waytsill left from the branch and dived down before flapping wildly towards the sound of the call. It was only a short distance to the nest from the central gun tree and Waytsill could instantly see the cat was engaged in a fight with a mytre. He didn't hesitate. He bombed directly into the fight.

-0-

The cat jumped into the nest, scaring each mytre half to death without striking a blow. The mytres reacted quickly and each began pecking the cat on its head mercilessly.

"Get out, be gone, vile cat," they each called as they struck out at the cat with their beaks and claws. The cat was now the one who was surprised by the ferocity of their response. She'd expected at least one bird to take flight as they had at the other nest, so she would only have to fight the remaining bird, or for both to take to flight so she could claim the nest and destroy any chicks that might be left behind.

However, both mature birds stayed to fight as a team. The cat took a moment to rearrange his plan and while he took some nasty blows to the head, none had done any long-lasting damage. She decided to focus on one bird – the slightly bigger male.

"Fly or die," the cat called as she swiped out at the male mytre's head.

"Get out of our nest," the female called back flapping her wings towards the invader.

The cat had not expected them to resist so forcefully, and she contemplated a retreat. Then she heard the male call, "You fly, my love, I'll fight the vermin."

Suddenly, Waytsill was at the lip of the nest, striking and slashing out at the cat.

"Fly, fly…" Waytsill was calling, to both mytre, "I'll hold the keere beast off."

The cat was suddenly facing three mytre and began to wonder again about a retreat. But before she could act, the female mytre took to wing, escaping the cat's blows, lifting away to a higher branch.

Waytsill stabbed at the cat's fore paws and face and tried to draw the attack away from the other male mytre.

Seeing she now faced just two birds the cat slashed the face of the male mytre and sank her teeth into the bird's throat. Instantly, the male mytre sank to the bottom of the nest, dead. Then, in a show of force and cruelty, she tossed the dead mytre over the lip of the nest and into the surrounding darkness. It landed at the base of the tree with a sickening thud.

Waytsill was stunned and flew back, away from the cat, beating his wings forcefully to fly away and up to the branch were the female mytre was watching. No sooner had Waytsill landed than the female mytre screamed and flew directly at the cat knocking her from the nest.

The cat fell past a few branches that snatched at the cat's flanks as she fell. She struggled to right herself as she tumbled, but with her legs and claws out, she managed to snag a small branch and swing back onto her feet before landing like a gymnast on a beam. She looked up at the female mytre now in possession of the nest.

"Go or die," the female mytre shouted through her tears and anguish.

"Go," she repeated, softly, "Go."

The cat could see the other mytre above her on the branch. *Maybe I'll find an easier nest to attack*, she thought, as she panted. Then, in a nonchalant almost dismissive manner, the cat turned, flicked her tail and hopped from branch to branch down the tree until she landed gracefully on the valley floor, a short distance from the mytre she had cast from the nest.

"Are you alright?" Waytsill called to the female mytre as he flew down and perched next to her on the lip of her nest.

"We should have left this valley," she said bitterly, "...this valley of death."

"Maybe," agreed Waytsill, "but we are here now and by Elppa's grace I will defend what I have, rather than wish for a place I have never seen."

Both birds were in shock at the loss of the male mytre, but they dare not fly down to land near the body until they were sure the cat had gone. But Waytsill wanted to see which way the cat had travelled, and he flew to a lower branch as he watched the cat leave. *West... towards where Elppa sets,* he thought. *We'll be ready for you next time cat.*

-0-

The cat walked west until she reached the creek. There she turned south, toward the valley road and after waiting for a carto pass, she rushed across the road and stealthily probed the former Wayt clan lands for more mytre to destroy.

-0-

Waytsill flew back up to the nest. "Come with me," he demanded, "it's not safe here, alone. If your able, and willing, you can join the flying squad and help protect other nests."

"To fight that killer keere cat?" she asked.

"That's what we do... when we find it," Waytsill replied.

"I'll come," said the female mytre with determination and resolve. "I'll kill that cat if it's the last thing I do. It killed my partner and defiled our nest. I swear I'll kill it."

Waytsill's own courage grew on the back of her resolve. "Come on then, we must warn the clan who have nests in the west that the cat maybe heading in their direction."

"First let me sing a lament for my partner so he will be helped into the Great Flock of Elppa. He was a brave and strong mytre of the former Krat clan." She paused and added, "and Valley Clan." Waytsill joined in with her sad and sweet chorus.

Quardle oodle ardle waddle doodle, oodle ardle waddle, they sang, lifting their voices into the darkness and gloom of Egnaro's domain. Around the valley, other mytre heard the lament and while none joined in, they all knew that it meant the cat had struck again.

"I am one of Lord Krat's children," she said when the song was over. "I'm Kratguna… now of the Valley Clan." She sounded sad but resolved to fight.

"I'm Waytsill," the younger mytre replied. And without another word, they flew, fast, firstly back to the central patrol tree to report back to Karnny. Then all three mytre took off to nests west of the creek to help guard them and give them a warning that the cat was coming.

-0-

There were two nests in Waytbill's home or nest tree. One was the nest he and Waytjulia had built for themselves and the one they had returned to after Lord Kratt's death. The other belonged to one of Waytbill and Waytjulia's children and her partner from the former Cor clan. They were tired and drawn, anxious and nervous from watching throughout Egnaro's dim darkness and listening to the sounds of battle that reached them from the eastern side of the valley.

Waytbill stood watch on one of the tree's higher branches. From there he could usually see up the valley and back across to the forest from where the lizard had come not many passages of

Egnaro before. But the low cloud and mist made it hard to see anything at all.

He imagined that the cat would also cast a shadow as it came, as the invading lizard had done, but he knew she was more cunning than the lizard and more silent and stealthier. He had heard the carolling and lament for a mytre being sung into the Great Flock and although he had no idea who it was, he knew the cat was about in the valley, and his blood practically froze.

Waytjulia was in the nest on their brood of two small chicks, and she knew her daughter and partner were only a few branches below her with their three chicks.

The low cloud bank had become a thick mist that hung like a shroud about the tree and Waytbill could see nothing more than the few branches about him. He soon recognised that staying on lookout was futile, so Waytbill flapped and flew down to his own nest and reassured Waytjulia that all seemed to be quiet.

The cat had crawled slowly across the ground, from bush to bush and shrub to tree. The mist that fell about her swirled as she moved and for a while she thought this alone would give her a way to sneak up and approach the tall nest tree - unseen. As she advanced, nothing cried out or signalled her coming and she came on silently toward the isolated tree.

The chicks were silent and an eery dread came with the coils of mists that drifted about the tree.

"Something feels foul," Waytbill whispered to his partner. Adding, "Pull the chicks in closer to your flanks." He could feel and hear his own heartbeat as he waited for what seemed like an age, for the mist to clear. But it came too late, and the cat was up the tree and ready to strike at the first nest before any of the mytre knew she was there.

The sly cat leapt into the lower nest striking one of the adult mytre across the back. The other mytre took immediately to flight and disappeared into the darkness within a heartbeat. The cat set upon the adult mytre scratching and biting it savagely until the mytre lay motionless in the nest. Then the cat killed the three small chicks cowering in the nest.

Waytbill's daughter flew rapidly in a wide ark and gathered speed as she flew. Then she barrelled in through the tree branches and hit the cat in the flank as it was in the process of tearing into the three chicks.

Taken by surprise the cat was winded and shocked as the blow landed. But the attacker had not knocked the cat from the nest and instead the invader had only been knocked onto the floor of the nest. There, the cat struggled for air as its side ached from the blow.

The mytre turned in an instant and dashed back into the nest with the aim of spearing the cat with her beak. It almost worked. But as Waytbill's daughter charged at the cat, Waytbill, who had heard the attack did the same. He dived from his nest above, to spear the cat as it tried to regain its breath and composure. Both mytre clashed mid-air and Waytbill was forced off balance and flew past the nest. His daughter speared right into the nest and the waiting cat.

The cat made sure to grab the mytre and hold her until her jaws and claws had sealed off the mytre's airway and crushed her vengeful attack.

Waytbill flew up to his nest and landed on a nearby branch. From there he could see into his daughter's nest below. There he saw the cat was now holding his daughter about the neck with its jaw. The bodies of the three chicks and his daughter's partner lay at the cat's feet, as his daughter's head fell to one side and her eyes closed.

"Keere, killer," Waytbill called at the top of his lungs. The cat released its grip on the bird and cowered down ready to strike should this other mytre attack. The cat's eyes blazed yellow and pale in Egnaro's gloom.

Waytbill peered back at his adversary with his pale brown eyes. Both looked resolute and determined, although Waytbill's eyes burned with rage as he took in the disaster that had overcome his kins nest.

"Nine lives," the cat said, cryptically as she moved away from the dead birds and strode out of the nest and onto the adjoining branch.

"Nine lives have I taken in this passage of Egnaro. With my return I'll take another nine until all the mytre are gone from this valley." The cat snarled and hissed as she spoke. Then, she crawled slowly along the branch, advancing one paw over the other, edging ever so slightly closer to Waytbill.

"Nine dead now, nine more to come, bird," the cat boasted as she continued to advance. The cat was aware of the damage she had done but she had sustained some injuries too. Her head hurt, as did her side where the last mytre had struck her. After having been at work in the chicken coop during the last past passage of Egnaro, she felt suddenly tired.

"Stay back," Waytbill called as he followed the cat's every movement along the branch. "Leave my tree, or pay the price for your trespass, keere cat," he called.

The cat was content with her work and thought better of continuing the fight. *There is always the next Egnaro to do dark wicked deeds,* she thought. She stopped, sat up and as if sitting on the norzela nest windowsill, she began to lick the blood from her paws and claws and preen her fur. Confident in her killing powers, she ignored the mytre above her as she took pride in her prowess as a killer.

It was at this moment that Waytbill struck. He launched himself off his branch and flashed directly at the cat's face. He was a mature mytre in his prime and he had never taken his eyes off the cat's pale-yellow eyes. He plummeted for one now. Her right eye was closest and Waytbill struck it with his beak at terrific speed.

The cat was too focused on its preening and had almost no time to react. So it was that the full force of Waytbill's attack saw his beak sink deep into the cat's face and eye socket. Waytbill dived past the cat as he struck, pulling the cat's eye out as he did. Then he flew away into the shadow of the mist in the late glow of Egnaro before returning to his nest high in the tree.

The cat almost fell from the branch, but she managed to sink her claws into the wood and keep hold. Now badly injured, she let out a blood curdling cry, before jumping down the tree, branch to branch, and landing with a gentle thud on the ground. Her right eye was gone, and she scurried away back toward the sealed road.

Waytbill took to wing again, looping around behind the cat and harassing it as it fled. He dived at its rump as she leapt through the underbrush and mist of Egnaro's valley. Waytbill soon lost the fleeing keere killer and returned to his nest, Waytjulia and their two chicks.

Within a moment, Waytsill, Karnny and the female former Krat clan mytre, Kratguna, who had joined the flying squad arrived in response to the commotion south of the sealed road.

They were devastated to see the carnage in the nest, particularly Waytsill as this was his sister's nest. All the mytre joined in a lament, as they carolled and sang for their fallen mytre chicks and their brother and sister mytre to be taken into the Great Flock of Elppa.

"I took its eye," Waytbill said, "It'll think twice before coming back to my nest tree," he said defiantly.

"But it will come back, won't it," Kratguna said bitterly.

"Yes, it will, I am afraid," Waytbill said softly, "perhaps with more malice."

"Then... we have until it returns to get ready," Karnny said, adding, "I wish Cordelia were here."

PART 2
NINE LIVES AND TWO WINGS

12

THE VET

If we could talk to the animals, learn their languages
Think of all the things we could discuss
If we could walk with the animals, talk with the animals,
Grunt and squeak and squawk with the animals,
And they could squeak and squawk and speak and talk to us.

Rex Harrison – 'Talk to the Animals' (From Doctor Dolittle) –
(1967)

WHEN TRAN AND VAL had taken the injured Cordelia to the vet in the box Val had found for him. Tran had left the box with the receptionist who assured him the bird would be in good hands. Tran and Val looked pleased with themselves for deciding to bring the injured bird to the vet and as they turned to leave Tran said, "Call us if you need anything, otherwise we'll come back in a few days to collect the magpie."

"Or the vet can bring it out… oh…" said the receptionist, "what happened to the cat?"

"My daughter thought it would make a nice pet, we have a few hectares and while she has a small dog, I think she likes to collect pets," Val replied.

"Don't worry though, I'll get a bell and collar on the cat before we let it out of the house," Tran said. Adding, "It's in our house with my daughter now, but I will not let it out without a bell on."

"Good," said the receptionist, "stray cats do so much damage to native animals, as I'm sure you know." She paused and added, "We sell cat collars and bells here at the front desk if you want to get one from us." As she spoke, she looked across at Cordelia once more. *You're a lucky bird,* she thought as she opened the door for Tran and Val to leave.

"See you in a few days, bird," Val said as they left.

-0-

Later that afternoon, the vet looked at Cordelia's injured wing and as the x-ray didn't show any permanent damage, she strapped the injured wing to Cordelia's side.

"It will get better with rest," the vet said reassuringly to the bird. "The x-ray didn't show any long-term injury or bone damage." Then the vet placed Cordelia in a wire cage and closed the door. As he did his veterinary nurse came in to help him.

"It was good of them to bring in a wild bird," she suggested.

"Yer...most people would have left it," the vet concluded with a sigh.

"Yer, I guess, but I heard the bird was being attacked by a cat in the man's garden so maybe he felt responsible."

"Or," said the vet, "he just knew about the damage and danger cats pose to native Australian wildlife and he couldn't let it kill the poor thing."

The vet said to his nurse, "We'll look after it for a few days. The wing is strapped, but it will need to rest, and it will need a bit of TLC before getting back to the wild." The vet paused, then said, "I haven't seen a magpie with a tuft of feathers on its brow like this one though. Must be a special bird, a special marking or something," she speculated.

"It looks pretty healthy apart from the injured wing and the trauma of being attacked, though," his nurse suggested cheerily.

Cordelia dared not move. She was in great pain although her injured wing was strapped. This had happened before, she remembered, when she was on the station. She hoped that soon she would be able to fly again, as she'd done after her care there.

For now, she sat alone in the cage, surrounded by barking or crying dogs, and scratching meowing cats. She was unsure what might happen and how long she would be incarcerated in the strange cage that smelt of dog, cat and something else, something unnaturally clean, sterile and un-valley like. In fact, the whole room smelt of the disinfectant and cleaning solution that made the environment most unnatural, most un-wild. She hated being so close to the other creatures, particularly the cat and the strange dog. However, unable to fly or defend herself, she had little choice but to hope the strange new norzela were kind and would not harm her further.

Cordelia reassured herself, that given that she was in the cage, alone, she was likely to be safe, for now.

The vet's holding pens were in a room at the back of the veterinary clinic and there was a bank of cages and pens of various sizes. Cordelia was up high in a smaller pen. From her vantage point she could see most of the room, although the cages below her were hidden from her view.

Opposite, she could see that most of the cages were empty, apart from one with a truly huge dog, another that held two small cats, and another that held a strange animal, she'd not seen before. It was covered with fur and smelt of eucalyptus and was twice the size of any cat she had seen.

Koalas were once common the valley, but none lived there any longer and Cordelia had not seen one before.

The only other cage she could see held a small, pink creature. Like the grey fur covered beast, it seemed to be sleeping most of the time. Cordelia could see too that it had a strange red light shining on it through the bars of the cage.

"It's a piglet," the big dog said, noticing her looking at it inquisitively. "A runt. Too small to survive in the litter. It was brought here to be nursed independently," the dog offered, adding, "It has little hope..." then changing his tone to a more cheerful one, he added, "I'm Boxer...not a 'boxer', you understand, it's just that my name is Boxer. I'm..." He paused while he puffed up his massive chest, "a Great Dane."

Cordelia didn't understand much of what he'd said. She could see he was a dog of massive size, but she had no idea that dogs came in a variety called Boxer, so none of what Boxer said really made sense. Although, she knew the dog was being kind or at least polite and she appreciated his conversation.

"I'm Cordelia, a mytre of the valley. I was injured in a fight with a cat,' she explained. "What are the norzela like here?" she asked, "And where am I?"

"You're at the vets," Boxer replied. "They really look after you here. I come here often to have my nails trimmed, or to have my weight checked. Today I'm here for something called 'desexing'. My owner said, 'It was time I was 'desexed' and that the vet would take great care of me'. I am having an 'operation' or something, sometime soon, apparently."

"Will it hurt?" Cordelia asked, concerned.

"Oh no... why would my owner do anything to hurt me? I'm sure it's nothing really. 'Over in a flash', I heard the vet tell my norzela owner."

Cordelia grimaced as a spasm of pain ran through her wing to her shoulder. "I hope you don't have any pain like this shoulder of mine. It's become very stiff and sore," Cordelia replied as she shifted for comfort in the cage. As she spoke a vet nurse came in through the holding area door and after opening Boxer's cage she placed a lead on him. His tail began to wag wildly in anticipation of a walk. He knew that was what a lead usually meant... 'walkies'.

"Okay..." the vet nurse said, "good boy...time for the snip."

Cordelia watched him happily walk off with the vet nurse before she settled herself down to rest, as well as she could, with her sore wing. *I hope he's alright*, she thought, *the 'snip' doesn't sound all that appealing.*

The grey furry thing opened its eyes and slowly chewed on a small branch of eucalypt leaves. "I'm Kevin," the koala said with a mouth full of leaves. "I've been here since the fire. I was very badly burnt and the norzela here have been very kind to me. But I wish I could go home… I am far better than I was, and I miss my siblings and friends." Then without skipping a beat, he dropped off to sleep again. Still sitting in the junction of a branch that had been secured in his cage, and still with his mouth full of eucalypt leaves.

Cordelia shook her head in surprise and blinked as she tried to grasp what the strange animal said. The fire was many passages of Elppa ago. The flood, the lizard invasion and the arrival of the cat have all occurred since the fire passed through the valley. *I can't be here as long as this creature*, she thought. *The cat will have destroyed everything.*

-0-

The piglet squealed with delight as it ran about the cage. It ran from one side to the other and crashed into the wire cage and its food bowl. As it ran, it tore up the paper covering the bottom of the cage.

"So, you're awake, little one," Cordelia said as she watched with amusement as the tiny pink animal ran and jumped joyfully across the cage.

"I am," said the piglet. "Who are you? You're new."

"I'm Cordelia," she replied, "a mytre from the Valley Clan.

"Nice to meet you, Miss Cordelia," the piglet said, with one trotter folded back in as it bent to bow respectfully. "I don't know where I'm from, I was brought here before I even knew my mother and brothers and sisters or father. I think I'm a runt, but I don't know what that means."

"It means you are a very special animal," Cordelia suggested, "So special, you were brought here to be cared for and raised with very special care."

"I'm special?" the piglet gushed.

"Do you have a name little one?" Cordelia asked.

The piglet stopped running and stood still on her tiny trotters and stiff little legs before she said, "I don't know, they, the norzela, just call me Runt!"

"Oh, that won't do… you'll need a proper name so you can find your place in the world," Cordelia explained. "Now, what sort of name should you have?"

"Can I pick my own name?" the piglet asked excitedly.

I don't see why not, Cordelia thought, "Certainly, little one," she replied. The piglet let out a cry of joy and ran across the cage.

He stopped and propped and, looking up at Cordelia, he called out, "I'd like to be called… Dash." Then without waiting for a reply he tore off to run a lap of the cage again.

Dash, thought Cordelia, *what a wonderful name.*

"Dash, Dash, Dash," the piglet called, as he ran from one end of the cage to the other, tearing up newspaper and knocking scraps from his food bowl in the process.

"I'll never dash again," the large dog, Boxer said in a groggy slur.

"So, you're awake too," Cordelia sang.

"Awake but not the same… I've been mutilated," Boxer lamented with a howl.

"Gone, they took them, cut… snipped… gone. How will I ever be a man again?" Boxer howled between tears and whimpers.

A vet nurse came into the room and said, "What's going on here? Birds singing, dogs howling, little pigs squeaking and running about all over the place."

Boxer looked at the nurse and howled, "I thought we were going for a walk."

"There's a good boy," she said playfully.

"I am… I am… a good boy?" Boxer growled. "Or at least I was a boy… now what am I… I mean, am I a boy at all? You trickster. I'll give you good boy." With that he lunged at the bars of the cage and at the vet nurse beyond. She stepped back, surprised at the suddenness of the attack.

"You'll be calmer in a few days," she said, retreating from the room. Cordelia thought, *there's a cat I'd like to 'desex' back in the valley*. Then she realised she had no way of knowing where the valley was or how to get out of the cage.

"How can we get out of these cages?" Cordelia asked Boxer, and Dash.

"Get out?" Dash replied, "I like it here, it's warm, I'm fed, and they let me sleep or play all day."

"I'll get out when my owner comes to collect me," Boxer said, with certainty. "They love me, really, and while I don't understand this mutilation, I know they will come for me. I'm a vital part of their pack."

"I need to get back to the valley,' Cordelia said. "My family, my friends and my clan members need me to fight off a cat."

"A cat?" Boxer exclaimed, with a huff. "One of those little helpless, harmless things?" he said, gesturing to the two tiny sleepy cats in the cage to his right.

"They're not helpless or harmless in the wild," Cordelia replied, desperately, "and I am no help to my clan stuck here. I have to find a way to get home."

"Maybe you'll just have to accept that there are some things you can't control, Miss Cordelia," Boxer suggested. "I couldn't control the removal of my… my…" he could hardly speak. "My… oh it's too painful to say," Boxer howled again, before raising his leg and licking the suture line in his groin.

"I couldn't control being sent to live here away from my brothers, my sisters, my father or my mother," Dash added. "Maybe you will have to accept that you will be here for a while until you're better, until your wing has healed at least."

But when will that be? Cordelia thought.

"I wish I had my pack here," Boxer said. "I'd show that vet nurse what it means to be in a cage and missing your…" He paused, "You see, there was a time when we dogs were unstoppable. We lived in packs, groups, and we never stood alone, we always stood as a pack, as a collective, able to bring down the biggest foe or enemy as one pack. Alone, one dog might be a great fighter, but with a pack, no one dog can win, and all always conquer, if they work together.

"My mother always told me… packs win, if you stand with kin." But alone I have to accept my fate. Alone I am not strong enough to stand against the norzela, so I become part of their pack and that way I am never really alone." Boxer returned to his wound care licking.

As Cordelia pondered what Boxer had said a plan began to formulate in Cordelia's mind. *But first I have to escape this cage,* she thought.

13

RESURRECTION

Sometimes I lead, sometimes I follow
This time I'll go where she wants me to go
She said maybe today, maybe tomorrow
Deep in the woods down the low valley road
While no one was lookin' on the old plantation
He took her all the way down the long valley road
They sent her away not too much later
And left him walking down the old valley road
Walk on
Walk on, walk on alone
Walk on, walk on
Walk on alone, alone

Bruce Hornsby & The Range – 'The Valley Road' (1988)

TIME PASSED SLOWLY at the vets. Boxer had gone, collected as he'd said by his norzela pack. The piglet was still there, running about and dashing as far as he could in the confines of the cage. All Cordelia could do was rest in her cage and watch the piglet scurry about. She could feel her wing was stronger and she knew that if the binding was removed, she could fly. But first the binding needed to be removed, and the cage door opened. *Then? Then what?* she thought. *Again, I don't know where I am or how to get home, back to the valley.* She felt wretched, bleak even, and she was becoming more despondent with each passing of Elppa.

She was sure that Elppa had risen and gone at least three times, but it was difficult to estimate in the confines of the cage, in the storeroom at the back of the vets.

The grey furry koala, Kevin, had advised her to sleep and rest as much as she could. "This way you'll save energy, and the time will pass peacefully."

Cordelia had tried to sleep, but sleep came to her only briefly with worry and anxiety clouding each passing of Egnaro. When she did sleep her dreams and visions were cold and disturbed. She saw nests full of blood, dead mytre laying at the base of trees, chicks torn and mutilated. Death, mist, and anguished cries filled her mind, and it seemed, the valley. Not knowing what was occurring in the valley meant her mind invented outcomes and filled in the blanks with visions of disasters, loss, and heartache.

The only thing she was sure of was that her partner, her two chicks and brother Corxell were still alive. Nothing in her dreams or visions had revealed to her that any significant harm had come to them. Although a cloud, like the one that had come to the valley during Egnaro's passage, hung over her vision of her mother, Corselia. She was alive, she sensed this, but there was a veil of dread that gripped Cordelia's mind when she tried to see her mother.

-0-

At the end of the third passing of Egnaro since Cordelia had been captured, a new bird was admitted to a cage in the storage room. It was a galah, with grey wings and a vest of pink. It was a young male, with a smooth scalp of white feathers. Cordelia saw the bird arrive and waited for it to rest before asking who it was, and why it was in the cage.

"I'm Goth," the injured bird said as it winced in pain. "I was attacked by a cat near the road that runs through the valley not far from here."

Immediately Cordelia was alert, and she sent a barrage of questions in the direction of the small grey-pink bird. "Where were you attacked, exactly."

"Near the sealed road, just as it runs over a creek," Goth replied.

"When?"

"Just as Elppa rose… I was feeding in the tall grass at the side of the road when a cat came running across the road and barrelled into me. Without warning or reason, it started to attack me, biting and scratching at my wing and clawing at my back. I was lucky because a car came along at just that moment and stopped to help me and halt the attack. It scared the cat away before it could kill me, but I was left unable to fly and the norzela brought me here in their car. Another norzela strapped my wing and then put me in here. Do you know where I am?" Goth concluded.

"It's called a vets'," Cordelia said, "They are norzela who, I think, care for injured animals… but what happened to the cat?" Cordelia snapped.

"Oh… I don't know, it ran off as soon as the norzela appeared. It was odd though; the cat only had one eye. Its right eye had been plucked from its face and blood covered its cheek and face. Horrible it was." The galah settled down to rest, before saying, "Been a heck of a time. Elppa acts in very strange ways sometimes. I'd only stopped for a quick feed too."

"Were you in 'the' valley when you were attacked?" Cordelia asked, excitedly.

"'The valley?" The galah pondered. "Could h've bin I guess, I've not been around here long, and I am still learning where is where and what is what."

If it was the valley and this was the same cat, then it has been fighting with mytre, and it is injured. But at what cost, Cordelia thought. *I really need to get out of here.*

-0-

"We need an elpitlum," Waytbill suggested. "We need to know what damage the cat has done and how we can better manage the keere cat's attacks.

"I agree," Barry said, "but where in the valley is safe to meet if we don't know where the cat is?"

"It's injured and it might have found a place to hide to lick it's wounds," Waytbill said.

'But we don't know if it has gone to lick it's wounds or where it could be hiding… nowhere in the valley is safe," Barry repeated, hotly.

"We shouldn't meet on the ground," Karnny said, knowing that mytre had always met to make decisions on the ground. "We should meet in Barry's old nest tree where Corselia is, or at the central flying squad tree. At least these trees are big enough for all the birds of the elpitlum to gather in one place and they are high off the ground, so we should be safe."

"Nowhere is safe," put in Kratguna with a tone of bitterness and grief.

"Nowhere is safe if we don't formulate a strategy to beat this cat," Waytbill said sternly. "So, we need to meet, soon and before the coming Egnaro."

"Come to the old nest tree I shared with Cordelia," Barry said, sadly, "I can bring the two chicks to see Corselia at the same time.

"Karnny, and Waytsill can spread the word," Waytbill proposed.

"I can help too, if this is the decision of the Valley Clan leadership," Kratguna offered. Waytsill nodded his appreciation. Then they all bid each other farewell.

"Until we meet at the tree elpitlum," Waytbill declared, in a whisper.

-0-

The vet came in and took Cordelia from the small cage. Cordelia saw her opportunity to escape, and she began flapping her wings as soon as the bandage was removed. The vet held the bird firmly and marvelled at its energy and ferocious flapping, but she held on tightly before placing the bird in a smaller carry cage.

Some birds just can't wait to get back into the sky, the vet thought as she closed the clasp on the travel cage. "Come on bird, let's get you back to your home territory," the vet said. Cordelia had no idea what was going to happen, and she flapped and called out a farewell chorus to Dash and Kevin, and the new galah, Goth."

"Vanquish the cat," Goth called as Cordelia was carried out of the room full of cages, to the vet's car. The vet placed the cage on the back seat and got in the driver's seat. After starting the car, the vet said again, "Okay, bird, let's get you back home."

Cordelia had understood none of what the norzela said, but there was something reassuring in the vet's voice that helped Cordelia relax and even enjoy her third ride in a car. The afternoon was drawing to a close by the time the vet's car rolled into Tran's driveway.

-0-

The cat had returned to the native mint bush in Tran's front yard, near the lawn. There she was shielded from view, and she felt safe. Her eye socket was very sore, and her vision somewhat limited. But she thought, *I'll get that bird, his partner and his chicks, before Egnaro's passage is over.* The cat spent the day resting and licking her paw so she could run the fur over the vacant eye socket. As the day wore on, the pain eased, and the blood was cleared from her paws and face. Elppa broke through the clouds at times, and the lightly flowered native mint bush offered a warm and dry place for the cat to rest and plan her next adventures with the coming of Egnaro.

-0-

"Hi Tran, Val," the vet said, as she put the travel cage down, adding, "Is this where you rescued the bird?"

"On the lawn, there," Tran pointed. The vet carried the cage over to the lawn and said, "Do you want to do the honours?"

"What... let the bird go," Val confirmed.

"Yer, you helped rescue it from the cat. Come to think of it, I wonder if it was the same cat that destroyed your chickens?"

"It may have been," Tran replied, "We haven't seen it since we let it go the other night, and I found this in the chicken pen today," Tran said, holding up the bell and collar.

"Looks like the cat really was the culprit."

"I don't sup'ose I can borrow that cage there, to try and trap the fiendish feline?" Tran asked.

"You can borrow it for a few days, but I doubt you'll have much success. These feral cats are as cunning as church rats," the vet suggested. "But… " she added, "knock yourself out, as long as you bring the cage back in one piece before the end of the week. Frankly I have had some other wildlife injured by feral cats lately and if you can catch one, that will help the local native animals tremendously."

"Deal," Tran said with a smile, adding, "Come on luv, get the bird out so I can get the cat in." Val bent over the cage and looked at Cordelia. "This bird has a funny little tuft of feathers over its beak. Is it a new breed of magpie?" she asked the vet.

"Just a special bird… I think," the vet replied. Val took the clasp off the cage door and opened the cage, looping a clip of wire around the open door so she could step back and allow the bird to exit of its own accord. Finally, Cordelia was free to go.

-0-

Cordelia looked around at each of the three norzela. *Could this be a trick?* she wondered. The norzela all stepped back and seemed to be waving at her to leave the cage. There was no line of mincemeat like there had been at the last cage she had been encouraged from. But she recognised the lawn and could hear Jock barking excitedly, near the norzela nest. This was the valley she knew, and she could hardly believe her good fortune at being returned to the place she knew as home.

Then she saw the cat curled up under a low hanging bush with purple flowers and drooping stems, near the norzela nest driveway. Cordelia felt rested and strong, but she hesitated a moment before stepping out onto the lawn. The cat looked to be asleep and had not seen her or woken to look at the norzela on the lawn. Cordelia could see it was the same ginger cat, but there was something different... she looked carefully... and saw that one eye was missing. This was the same cat that had attacked Goth. This was the same cat that had attacked her and come to terrorise their valley. Rage boiled inside her. Rage and determination.

Cordelia took her time. First, she stood tall on her legs. Then she flapped her wings, giving them a full and vigorous stretch, before stepping once, twice and launching into the late Elppa's air. Within a wing beat she was rising, up into the air. Making a bee line for her old nest tree. Feelings of rage passed as her determination grew. All she could think of was flight, freedom, Barry, her chicks; Vall and Valora, Corselia, Corxell, the Valley Clan, and how she would unite the clan to banish the cat. Then, remembering her dreams, she thought about what might have happened while she'd been gone. There was no time to lose.

14

CORSELIA'S FLIGHT

We didn't start the fire
It was always burning
Since the world's been turning
We didn't start the fire
No, we didn't light it
But we tried to fight it

Billy Joel – 'We Didn't Start the Fire' (1989)

CORDELIA FLEW rapidly into the gathered throng of mytre. Many took to wing, thinking it was an invasion or attack, so quickly had her entrance been. Others protested loudly and demanded to know the meaning of the intrusion. Others, including Barry, Karnny, Kratguna, and Waytbill braced to attack and would have done so if Cordelia had not said immediately, "I'm sorry I was taken, but I'm back now."

A chorus of excited, relived, delighted and stunned mytre rose from the gathered birds and soon those who had fled returned to the nest tree to resume the elpitlum.

Cordelia was at once submitted to an avalanche of affectionate hugs as mytre rushed to greet her and rejoice at her return. Then she was swamped by a host of questions, fired at her from all sides.

"Where have you been?"

"Are you alright?"

"Why have you been away"

"Are you hurt?"

Cordelia held up her wings and said, "I'll answer everything, in time, and honestly, but first, Barry are you and the young ones safe?"

Barry was already at his partner's side, and they held each other in a tight hug, wrapping their wings about each other while sighing with relief.

"Thank Elppa your safe," Barry said, adding, "look they have fledged, Vall and Valora can fly."

"It's amazing," Cordelia said, as they too flew over for a hug. She was quietly disappointed to have missed their milestone, but she could see they were growing well and that Barry had clearly stepped up in her absence.

"Thank Elppa you are both safe," Cordelia exclaimed, as she hugged them again.

Karnny was overjoyed and said, "I told you she wasn't dead."

"Dead, no I wasn't dead, I was injured and taken by some norzela to be healed."

"Thank Elppa," Karnny said over and over.

"I'd thank the norzela," Cordelia said, "it was their kindness that saved me."

Then Cordelia addressed the gathered mytre. "There's no time to waste. We must attack the cat. It's by the norzela nest."

"We can't," Waytbill said sadly, "we were just about to leave, to find another home."

"What?" Cordelia said incredulously. "Leave... why?"

"The cat has been on a rampage and killed a large number of Valley Clan mytre and chicks. I took its eye, but it is too strong and too deadly for any of the mytre here to kill." As he spoke, Waytbill sounded tired, defeated and filled with grief.

"And this is what you want?" Cordelia asked Waytbill.

"No… I would stay and fight, but the clan has spoken…"

"Well, I'm part of the clan and I haven't had my say…" she hesitated, "and what are the thoughts of Corxell, Karnny, and Corselia?"

Karnny hung his head in defeat and said with a sigh, "We have fought the cat, and it has proven too strong. We have no choice but to leave before it destroys us all."

Cordelia looked around at the gathered mytre. They all looked tired, and worn, grief stricken, and lost. Corxell flew over to Cordelia and said, "We have to go, now…" He hesitated and Cordelia could see he was becoming tearful.

"Now?" She asked. He couldn't speak.

"While you were away," Karnny began, "Well, you knew that Corselia had been injured fighting the cat…"

Cordelia looked stunned in anticipation of what he was about to say. "Not Corselia… not mother… not now…" she stammered.

"She was healing a little, but when she thought you had died, she lost hope. Her heart broke and she lost interest in flight, fight, and food. She just drifted, into the Great Flock. She passed over only a short while before your return."

Corxell wiped some tears from his eyes, and finding his voice he explained. "We were just about to sing her onto her next journey when you arrived home." Corxell's tears fell freely as he told Cordelia about her mother's passing.

"I didn't see it,' Cordelia said, "I saw the cat, and the destruction, I saw the valley and our home, but not my mother's passing." Cordelia felt weak, and she held onto Barry as she steadied herself.

"We were about to sing Corselia into the Great Flock when you arrived," Waytbill repeated, "then we were going to leave the valley."

A number of the mytre began the chorus and the sound of, *'Quardle oodle ardle*…began.

"No…" Cordelia cried. "No… I don't want to go… I want to fight. I want to be rid of the keere cat and live here in peace… in our valley. What will Corselia have died for if we leave?" She paused, "What will any of the mytre killed by the cat have died for if we just leave?" Cordelia looked around at her stunned valley mytre and saw their heads fall and their eyes drop from her gaze.

"How?" Waytbill asked. "We have tried to fight, we have used the flying squad, we have fought and we have died. The cat is too keere and too strong."

"Maybe your friendly eagle could help," Karnny suggested, brightly, to Cordelia.

The thought had occurred to Cordelia, but it would mean a long and dangerous flight, and it would take days to reach the far mountains of the west. She didn't look confident, and she had chicks now. How could she abandon them again? They might be attacked at any time, and she would need to be here to defend them. She didn't respond and a cloak of gloom settled over the elpitlum.

Barry was unhappy with Karnny's proposal as the idea of Cordelia flying away after her recent return only made him feel ill and nervous. "How can you expect to find Gary when you have never been to his mountains," he asked, bitterly, "What if you are attacked on the journey. It's too dangerous, my love," Barry protested.

"I know it's a long way and I am not clear where to go…" she hesitated, "It's why I will not seek out Gary the eagle. He is not the answer we seek."

Many of the gathered mytre looked confused. Some mumbled about "weak leadership," and other said, "I thought we were singing Corselia into the Great Flock, then leaving."

Then Cordelia called out, "I have another plan for ridding the valley of the cat. Will you at least hear me before we sing and leave?"

No one else spoke for a long while. Some mytre whispered to their neighbours but the majority waited to see which way the elpitlum would fly.

"I will hear you, Cordelia," Kratguna called out. "My partner was killed by the cat last Egnaro and I will stay and fight if there is any chance to rid the keere beast from the valley."

"I'll fight too," another mytre called.

"Though I am tired and worn out I'll fight on," Karnny said defiantly.

"And me," said another mytre.

Cordelia looked at Waytbill, Waytjulia, Corxell and Barry. They all looked emotionally drained, worn thin and burdened by weariness, but each slowly nodded their approval.

-0-

Tran watched the mytre fly off to the east, then shook the vet's hand. "Thanks for all your help, mate. I'll give the trap a try and send it back in a few days if I have no luck."

"Maybe, put it over by the chicken coop," the vet suggested. "The cat's been there once before so it may be as good a spot as any other."

Tran picked up the cage, and he and Val watched as she drove away. Val walked over to Jock and gave him a little scratch behind the ears. As she did, Tran picked up the cage and walked with it over to the recently cleaned coop just beyond the lawn. He put the cage down by one of the wire walls and secured it to the coop with a few twists of wire.

Then he opened the cage door and propped it open with a slender stick. He had never set a cat trap before and while this effort was likely to be unsuccessful, he reassured himself that he'd tried and that it was very unlikely that the cat would come back in any case.

Tran walked back to the house and stopped to give Jock a gentle tickle behind the ears. "I'm sorry I thought you could have killed all those chickens, mate," Tran said kindly.

He took the chain off the hook and released Jock from his bonds. "Good dog," he said, before going inside. Jock could hear Val call out, "Make sure you wipe your feet, luv." Then Jock sat on the back step to keep a look out for the troublesome cat. He could smell it was nearby. And there was something else he could smell, *blood*, he thought.

-0-

Cordelia's plan had grown from something Boxer said while she was in the vet's cage. The pack is stronger than any one individual. *It would be by working as one pack that they could defeat the cat*, Cordelia thought.

Cordelia perched where the other mytre of the Valley Clan could see her and explained her plan.

"The only way to beat the cat is if we all attack at once, as a pack, as the Valley Clan. The cat can beat one or two or three mytre but if we all attack as a flock, a pack, we can drive it away or even kill it. For this plan to work we will all need to trust each other, and work as a team. The flying squad have been taught a special attack strategy that they will employ first. It's called the 'swoop, snatch, swing, spring, and sail' attack and Karnny, Corxell, Barry, and Waytsill will all use it to attack and drive the cat before them. Then every other mytre of the valley with maturity, will swoop in behind me and peck and push the cat away, and out of the valley. By the time we are finished with it, it will be the cat who is looking for a new place to live, not us."

Barry clicked his beak with Cordelia's in a show of support. "I'll fight my love," he said.

"I am here for the Valley Clan," Cordelia said, proudly, "for my young, for my family and my friends. For all the Valley Clan. This is our valley. We fought Lord Kratt, the fire, the flood, the lizard. We have chicks and we have friends here in this valley. My spirit is here, and my mother and father have died here, defending this valley. I'm proud of my clan. I'm proud of my friends, my spirit, our spirit is here... and I know how we can beat the cat... together."

"Together," Barry repeated. All the Valley Clan joined in a chant of, "Together... together... together."

Cordelia knew now that there was at least a little hope and she said, "I have learnt that the shortest flight to empowerment is the path we fly ourselves, but if we all fly as one, we will have a power that no cat can oppose... fly with me now...defend your valley, vanquish the cat."

15

TOGETHER

Captain & Tennille – 'Love Will Keep Us Together' (1975)

THE CAT HAD slept longer than she had planned. Pain, and two nights of activity had taken their toll. Elppa was low in the sky, but still a bright orange glow fell about the valley. Tran and Val loved this time of day, and they had come to their back veranda to watch the sunset.

"Peaceful isn't it, luv?" Val said, as she sipped a cup of tea.

"It's the best reason to have moved out of town. Can you hear that, luv?" He asked.

"No," she said, confused.

"Exactly… serenity and the peace of nature," Tran replied, with a smile. Tran surveyed the back garden, the lawn was tidy and cut, the driveway was tidy, with small white stones raked into a neat ribbon that ran along-side the house. The row of six mint bushes with their pink-purple flowers made a spray of colour against the green lawn and white driveway. Then he saw it.

"It's that bloody ginger cat," Tran exclaimed in disgust, "It's bloody well come back." Tran stood but was unsure what to do next.

"Leave it, luv," Val said, "let the cage catch it."

Tran sat back down, and said, "But the bloody cheek of it. To be just sitting their preening itself on our lawn, like it owns the bloody place."

Suddenly, their peace was broken as a flock of birds circled overhead crying out with a dreadful cacophony of sound.

"They're magpies, aren't they?" Val exclaimed, surprised.

"Yer… but I've never seen them in a flock like that before, normally you only see a few or a handful at once, I've never seen this many in one flock." Tran stood again as he took in the spectacle.

The cat saw the flock as they swooped and dipped above the norzela nest. Like Tran, she was transfixed by the swirling aerial convoy of mytre. Cordelia led the train of mytre as they dived at their target.

"Attack," she cried, 'Drive the cat away."

With that order, Karnny dived like a Stuka, directly at the baffled cat and unleashed a small log of wood about half his own size. It fell directly on target and struck the cat on the head.

"Me…ow," the cat cried in response to the strike. She was immediately hit by a second log as Corxell copied Karnny's dive and unloaded another blow to the cat's head.

"Ohooow," the ginger ninja cried.

This was followed by two more hits, one from Waytsill and one from Barry who managed to land his log a short way in front of the cat so that his log bounced once before striking the unhappy cat in the belly. The cat had no reply for this sort of intense bombardment. She turned and bounded over to the western end of the lawn. Karnny had found another weapon and in his second run unloaded a small stone hitting the cat on the right paw as it lifted it to protect her head.

"Me owooo," she cried again as pain rippled through her paw.

"Stand and fight," the cat called to the swooping mytre as they flashed past her face. She was not expecting the next phase of the mytre assault. Suddenly, the bombing stopped and the mytre, again led by Cordelia, dived claws or beak to the fore, directly at the cat's face.

"Aim for the good eye," Cordelia called as she sped at the cat. Exposed on the lawn the cat was an easy target, and she looked for a place to hide. The native mint bush was an obvious choice, and she thought about returning there, but it meant crossing back over the lawn and the cat thought better of exposing herself to a greater onslaught on the way.

Retreat, she thought, was her best option. Retreat into the natural part of the garden were there was a tall gum tree and a few other low bushes, wild grasses and the chicken coop to hide nearby. Although, as she turned to flee, the real onslaught of attacking mytre began. Cordelia had instructed all the mature mytre of the valley to follow her lead and swoop and dive with perfect co-ordinated timing. Cordelia dived and pecked or clawed at the cat, then the following mytre repeated the attack without a second's relief for her to recover or get its bearings. Mytre after mytre flew at the cat, striking with their beaks, scratching with their claws and always pushing the cat back off the lawn and down to the soil near the chicken coop.

The cat had no answer to the barrage of beaks and crescendo of claws. Many hit home and the cat was getting repeated blows to her head and around her only good eye. Her blind side made it harder to anticipate where the blows were coming from and she often didn't even see the blow until it had landed.

"Keep it up," Cordelia called. Adding, "Karnny, Waytsill, and Barry join in the rolling barrage. Keep the pressure on. Keep pushing the cat away."

-0-

Tran and Val were gobsmacked as they watched the poor cat being driven mercilessly across their back garden. "The cat's got no hope against the birds," Val called to Tran above the din of the bird calls and cat wails. Jock had started to bark his encouragement of the mytre attack, and the peace of the late Elppa's glow had evaporated before their eyes.

"What's going on?" Tran asked, stunned.

"It's a birdnado I think," Val said, "A bloody birdnado." Val had also risen from her chair to get a better view of the torrent of birds swooping and stabbing at the cat.

Jock barked in excitement and decided to join in the attack. Snapping and yapping close to the cat as the mytre flew sortie after sortie at their adversary.

The cat had suffered terribly under the avalanche of beaks and claws and was sure now that her only option was a speedy and complete retreat. She knew she might be safe in the chicken coop but also knew she would be too exposed while she tried to get in through the wire top. Then she saw the cage near the side of the chicken coop. *There*, she thought, *they can't get me if I am undercover in the cage.*

She recalled seeing a similar cage on the escarpment shelf, with the big lizard and the two foolish ravens. It had been used as a cage to keep their captives, but the cat knew it was also a good place to stay safe away from the flocking mytre.

Without a second thought, she dashed in through the open door of the cage.

As the cat did, Jock chased after her and knocked the slender stick making the cage door swing shut behind the cat and capturing her safely inside.

Mytre continued to crash into the side of the wire cage, as the cat cowered inside, until Cordelia called a halt to the assault.

"She's beaten," Cordelia called, adding, "gather... land on the lawn." Again she, with Barry at her side, glided down to the lawn and waited for the flock of mytre to land and come to stand in a tight circle around her.

"Now the cat is vanquished, it's time to sing my mother into the Great Flock of Elppa and celebrate your victory, together, over the cat," she shouted above the excited mytre gathered on the lawn. Cordelia threw her head back and called to her kin and friends, "Lift your voices and sing as Elppa's rays dwindle in the west."

As one, the mytre lifted their heads and cleared their throats to sing as no flock have ever sung before... *Quardle oodle ardle waddle doodle, ardle waddle, doodle...*

Jock ran onto the lawn and joined in, barking his respects to Cordelia's mother, Corselia. As they sang and barked, Elppa finally sank over the western hills of the valley. Tran and Val stood with their mouths open, enjoying the spectacle of a large mytre flock, singing one of their own into the Great Flock of Elppa.

16

AN ENCHANTED MOMENT

There's a calm surrender to the rush of day
When the heat of a rolling wind can be turned away
An enchanted moment, and it sees me through
It's enough for this restless warrior just to be with you

Elton John – 'Can You Feel the Love Tonight' (1994)

TRAN AND VAL watched as the magpies took off and flew away to the east into the growing darkness, as the sun finally set.

"Bloody hell, what was that?" Tran asked Val as he scratched his head.

"I don't know," she replied, "It looked like a magpie church service if you ask me. Whatever it was, it was bloomin' amazing," she concluded.

"Let's check the cage," Tran suggested as he hopped up and strode over to the chicken coop. He reached down and made sure the clasp on the cage was shut and that the cat really was ensconced within. The cat was quaking in the tray of the cage, with its paws over its head, and its tail under its belly.

"I'm gun'a take the cat to the vets right away," Tran said. "She won't believe we've caught it."

"I don't believe it... and I saw it," Val said, with a chuckle.

"What'll happen to it?" Val asked.

"Dun'o… might have to put it down, I reckon," Tran proposed. "After all, it killed all your chickens and my alarm clock," he reminded Val.

"S'pose…" she agreed, adding, "do you want a hand with it?"

"Nar," Tran said, cheerily, "she'll be right. I'll drive the bugger in to the vet's now… n' I'll be home for tea."

-0-

Cordelia led the triumphant mytre back to the nest tree. Their victory had been a marvel. Few of the mytre who took off in support of Cordelia's plan really believed it had any chance of success. But it had worked and all the mytre celebrated with singing and carolling as Egnaro rose well above the valley. The sky was clear and all Egnaro's children, the stars, shone with joy at the mytre's victory. Waytbill, Waytjulia, and Waytsill stayed only a short time.

"We have chicks to return to, and a nest in a tree we've known all our lives, thanks to you, Cordelia," Waytbill said with gratitude and kindness.

"Elppa's blessing on you," Waytjulia added.

"I want to stay in the old Cor clan nest tree, in my mother's old nest," Corxell said.

Cordelia knew the ghost gum nest tree had been his home too and she said, "I'd be proud to be your neighbour when we move the chicks back to our original nest. But we'll stay in the nest by the norzela park tonight. After the drama of the battle, I just need a place to sleep with my family around."

Karnny was still buzzing with excitement after the fight and he came to Cordelia and said, "I'm glad your back, I knew you'd return. I said you would… didn't I, Barry… I said, 'she'll be back', but no one believed me…no one."

"You did," Barry agreed, cheerily.

"Will we get the scout patrols up and running again?" Karnny asked, "Because I think Kratguna here would be a wonderful

116

addition to the squad… have you met her, she lost her partner recently to the cat and well, she is a terrific fighter… anyway."

"With Elppa's light, Karnny," Cordelia said, gently. "We can discuss the patrols with Elppa's light. I'll meet Kratguna then too. However, I'll need to rest first."

"Okay," Karnny said, taking the hint.

"With Elppa's light then." Other mytre also recognised the stress and weariness of the past few passages of Elppa growing on their bones and started to fly back to their own nest trees, chicks and families. As the ghost gum nest tree started to empty, Barry led Cordelia in a flight over to their chicks in the tall pine tree by the norzela park. The four mytre huddled close in the nest as they each thanked Elppa for Cordelia's safe return and the success of their cat attack. The chicks were excited but tired and they were soon asleep.

Then Barry told Cordelia about the way the cat had terrorised the valley while she'd been gone. "You can see why many of the clan wanted to leave," Barry explained. "It's a miracle you came back at all. Let alone when you did, because if you'd come a day later, it's possible the whole Valley Clan would have moved on to another place to live."

"It wasn't a miracle," Cordelia said, "it was Elppa's will. I had seen it in my dreams, and I knew I'd come back to the valley and find you and the chicks safe. Now we have to find a way to build a stronger clan, and ways to protect all the chicks and families of the valley."

"You've been through so much, my love," Barry said, as he nuzzled his beak into her throat.

"The Gods give us wind so we can fly, water so we can drink, darkness so we can sleep and Elppa gives us warmth and light so we can hunt and build our nests. Love," she said, "love… we have to find for ourselves, and remember, the shortest flight to empowerment, is the path we fly ourselves. The Gods give and take, but the choices we make are always ours."

"Truly, my dear you are as wise, kind, and gracious as the Cordelia from myth," Barry said, as they rested, together again.

-0-

Tran woke early. He had a lot to do as he was going to get Val some new hens and a new rooster. A week had passed since he'd taken the feral cat to the vets to be disposed of. The valley seemed to have returned to a place of peace and calm, even Jock seemed to be more settled, sleeping more and barking less.

Val was sorry the cat had been destroyed, but she understood the delicate balance of the Australian bush and knew the feral cat had no place in it. She was even surprised that Bree didn't mind the cat was gone. "I like Jock better," she said. "He doesn't scratch me."

With spring rolling into summer, Tran and Val found themselves enjoying more and more of the setting sun, as they sat on their back veranda and watched the evening rolled in. "That magpie's back," Val said, pointing to a black and white bird on their lawn. "The strange one with the little tuft of feather on its brow," she clarified.

Tran looked over at the bird. "I think it has a nest in the ghost gum along the driveway," he suggested, "and a family too," he added as three other magpies landed on the lawn next to Cordelia.

"They must be her partner and their two chicks," Val speculated. The four birds ignored the norzela and strode about the damp lawn stamping their feet or driving their beaks into the turf, searching for worms or grubs.

"One day I'll catch your tail," Jock called over from his cosy kennel without getting up to greet the mytre.

"One day... maybe," Cordelia called back.

"You know I think they are talking to our little dog," Val said with a smile.

"Nar, just natural for a dog to bark at a bird, isn't it," Tran said. "Beautiful bird the magpie..." he concluded, "just beautiful."

PART 3
THE GREAT FLOCK OF ELPPA

17

PEACE

When I die and they lay me to rest
Gonna go to the place that's the best
When I lay me down to die
Goin' up to the spirit in the sky

Goin' up to the spirit in the sky (Spirit in the sky)
That's where I'm gonna go when I die (When I die)
When I die and they lay me to rest
I'm gonna go to the place that's the best

Norman Greenbaum – 'Spirit in the Sky' (1969)

FOLLOWING THE CAT'S defeat, the valley slowly returned to a peacefulness they had only known briefly before the flood. Cordelia and Barry focused their attention on their chicks, Vall and Valora and the other valley mytre with chicks did the same.

All the deceased mytre were sung into Elppa's great flock and slowly the valley began to ring with the sounds of joy, as birds sang or carolled, and harmony bloomed along with the valley foliage. The scout flights remained and new young mytre were called into service so that all young mytre learnt the skills needed to keep the valley safe.

Cordelia knew it was essential that they kept up their scouting parties, but she also knew that even this might not be enough, and she called an elpitlum so that she could discuss an idea with the clan.

The idea was radical, and it took a long time to convince many of the less courageous mytre to agree to at least let her try the scheme. Even Waytbill, with his now fledged chicks was at first reluctant, but Cordelia convinced him that she needed to try her plan. Arguing that there was still a weakness in their valley's defence without something altogether more substantial to act as a deterrent or decisive weapon. Should another cat return, or in case another clan tried to infiltrate and take over their valley.

They spoke for a long time, with many mytre pointing out that the risks were too great, knowing what they all knew from their mytre history. However, Cordelia persisted speaking about a vison she'd had, years ago, before reminding them that her visions had been valuable in the past.

Barry asked, "Do any of you have another suggestion for keeping the valley safe and at peace?"

No one spoke, and for a long moment silence hung over the mytre gathering.

"At least let me try," Cordelia pleaded, "if it doesn't work, we've lost nothing."

-0-

Tran and Val settled into a routine of their own, as they grew to love their new home on the western valley side. Val's chicken's provided eggs and her garden grew to become a veritable cornucopia of vegetables and fruits, honey, and native flowers.

120

It took years for the garden she had envisaged, and both Tran and Val worked hard to foster a garden that was productive yet remained appropriate, suitable and sustainable, alongside the more common native vegetation spread richly throughout the rest of the valley.

-0-

Vall and Valora grew into fine young mytre, and before they left their nest tree and sought mates and families of their own, Cordelia had a proposal for them.

"I want to go and visit my friend, Gary, the eagle, in the western mountains," she suggested. "Barry and I have discussed it, and he is coming with me, but we'd like to know if you want to come too?"

"Away from the valley," Vall asked, unsure.

"With you both?" Valora clarified.

"Yes…" Barry put in. "It will be an adventure, and you will have your mother and I to help and guide you." He hesitated. "It will have its risks… but it'll allow you to see more of the world, and to know a little more about your mother's life and the challenges she faced."

"It will also help you build your confidence, and practice your flying and combat skills," Cordelia concluded. The two young mytre looked at their parents as if their beaks had fallen off.

"You're kidding… that would be amazing," Valora said, excitedly.

"Yer…totally awesome," Vall gushed.

"Then it's agreed… we'll fly as a family to the western mountains and search for Gary," Cordelia said, relieved that her two young mytre were coming.

-0-

They set off with the wind at their backs and found height as the western plains opened before them. Cordelia, who was far more

121

experienced at high level flying, flew over the others, watching out for predators or keere things and keeping the others in her sight. Barry who flew with the young mytre kept them distracted by telling them stories of their mother's adventures and the way the Valley Clan had come to fruition. They glided on updrafts and gyre that took them higher than they had ever flown before, but always Cordelia flew above them, making sure they were safe.

They passed over the green tree filled lands immediately west of the valley and were soon over open country with sparce scrubby bushes and long, undulating hills. They saw a road with norzela's cars racing along below them and occasional small towns or isolated buildings. They also saw frequent water filled dams sparkling under Elppa's light, but as they travelled further west, these like the trees of the valley, became less evident.

At one point a brown goshawk saw the three mytre flying together and was about to dive in an unopposed attack from above, when it was suddenly aware of a black and white bird at its wing.

"They are my kin," Cordelia said, with an authoritative tone. Adding, "I hope, hawk, you are not intending to attack them?" The goshawk saw the black feather tuft on Cordelia's brow and knew at once it was in the presence of Cordelia the brave, friend of Gary the wedge tail eagle, only son of Garth, grandson of Graham, great grandson of George, and descendant of the Great Gus, and the mytre who had humiliated it some years before at almost this exact place.

"No... Cordelia... the brave..." The hawk spluttered, before pausing to think... "I was just wondering why there are more mytre flying so high, and I was about to swoop down to ask them where they were going," the goshawk lied.

"We are going to the western mountains to visit the eagle Gary," Cordelia explained seeing immediately through the lie. "I hope you don't mind us passing through this area of sky... great and wise goshawk," she added.

"It's my pleasure to have you pass and to help guide you on your way, if you will allow me?" the goshawk said.

"That's most gracious," Cordelia said, surprised. "You are indeed a wise and gracious bird," Cordelia added, hoping her flattery would benefit them more than the risk of open conflict. She knew the hawk might stand little chance against the four mytre combined, but a safe passage and friendship were far more welcome, and she was glad the hawk was indeed a wise and gracious bird. They all flew on gliding down and flapping up, all the time moving west.

"There are the mountains you seek," the goshawk called to Cordelia as it swung around to fly back to its territory.

"Thank you," Cordelia called as they parted, "word will spread of your wisdom, hawk." As the goshawk flew away Cordelia glided down to Barry and the young.

"Not far now," she called out. "We'll stop at the station as Egnaro passes, then fly to the mountains with Elppa's light.

"Who was the bird that flew with you?" Barry asked.

"That was a goshawk who was about to attack you, but we had met before, and it recognised that grace was better than aggression. The hawk flew with me as a guide for a long while, but it's gone now." They flew on all together for a short while before Cordelia said, looking down, "I think that's the station." As she spoke, she nodded her head in the direction of a group of buildings, with their tin roofs glowing red in the final streaks of Elppa's light. "Come on follow me down."

-0-

Cordelia, Barry, Vall, and Valora all landed on the balustrade that surrounded the veranda. The outdoor setting seats the norzela had used were still there, although a small dust covered table now sat where the cage she had once been kept in had been. Immediately all four mytre started to carol.

Within a moment Bruce began to bark and dashed up to the back door asking to be let out.

"That's Bruce," Cordelia cried, excitedly. Then a norzela woman opened the back door and stood with her mouth open.

"It's the same magpie that was here before," she said, surprised. "Look it has the little tuft of feathers above its beak." She was followed out by Lilly and her father.

"Bloody hell," he said, as he scratched his head, "How did she find her way back here?"

"It's my magpie," Lilly shouted, causing Vall and Valora to jump into the air in fright.

"These must be her family," Mary said, recognising the two younger magpies as Cordelia's children. The four mytre continued their chorus as Bruce, who had finally been able to jump up on to one of the seats barked at Cordelia to come and greet him. Cordelia was overjoyed and flapped down on to the seat to play with the yappy chihuahua. Like old friends do, they fell into instant recognition as if they had spent no time apart at all.

"She even remembers Bruce," Mary said, "this really is a clever bird."

"I'll get them some food," Lilly said, as she went quickly back inside, and soon returned with a hand full of mince that she placed on the balustrade for each bird to peck and nibble at.

"I have come to find the eagle, Gary," Cordelia explained to Bruce. "I want him, and you, to meet my family...here is my partner Barry, and our two chicks Vall and Valora."

Barry cried out his greeting, while the chicks were more subdued in their acknowledgment, and also more focused on the mince.

"We've had a long flight, and we all need to rest now," Cordelia said, "but I want to talk with you, if you can?" she whispered. Bruce barked his understanding and agreed to meet with her before they left in the light of Elppa's glow.

"We'll roost at the old windmill as Egnaro passes, but I will return soon," Cordelia said. With that, all four mytre took to the wing and followed her out into one of the paddocks near the sheep shed and dipping yards, to sleep at the top of the windmill where she'd cared for Gary.

She was up early with Elppa's light and after their chorus to rejoice His return, Cordelia flew over to the norzela nest to find Bruce. Bruce was waiting. He'd heard their nwad chorus and knew it meant Cordelia would be with him soon and he was sitting paws crossed, on the veranda, awaiting her arrival.

"I missed you, Bruce, I'm sorry I had to leave so soon after your return from being ill. I know how close you came to dying at the jaws of that vile, keere, Yrarbil. I understand you were hurt and must have found it hard to forgive me. I'm so happy to see you well again, but I want to make it up to you. The day we stole the meat for the yard-dog, I promised that you could have your fill of meat from the slaughter shed. Today I have come back with my family to help make sure you get what I promised." She paused to allow Bruce time to take in what she was asking and offering.

Bruce was quick to respond, "No… no… since you left, I have never left the norzela nest or walked further than the lawn and fence that surround it. No…I couldn't go back there." Bruce began to withdraw back towards the back door and Cordelia could see he was visibly shaken by the prospect of returning to the shed, but she persisted.

"Bruce," she said softly and kindly, "you can't live all your life in fear of the shed or the long dead Yaribil we found inside. The worst thing I did that day was not just to keep my promise, but it was to allow that Yaribil to steal your courage and make your life small and diminished." She paused and watched as Bruce turned with the door to his back and sat on the door mat to listen.

"You deserve so much more than a life lived in fear," Cordelia sang. As she spoke, she stood tall on the balustrade and chorused out her words. "I promised you a meat feast and I will deliver it one way or another, but the meat will tase so much sweeter if you have the courage to come with me to the slaughter-shed and conquer your fear by joining my family there.

"Your family?" Bruce asked, "they are waiting there now?"

"They are," she clarified, "the meat tray is too heavy for one mytre to push, so my partner and my children will help me... if you'll come?"

Bruce was almost quivering with fear. *Still*, he thought, *she has come all this way to keep her promise. She is being helped by the kin to move the tray... for me... and the meat on the tray was indeed sweet and tender.* Bruce remembered the taste of the meat, how hard it had been to not eat it himself and to take it to the yard-dog. Now, Cordelia had returned to make sure she kept her word.

"I am afraid..." Bruce said, quietly, before adding, "however, I'll still come with you... I'll come and risk another encounter with a keere thing and my fears."

"I'll be with you, my friend," Cordelia reassured him. "You know a fear shared, is a fear halved." With Bruce's consent to take part, she took off across the station, flying for the slaughterhouse shed beyond the store shed. Bruce ran after her. He arrived outside the tall wooden door with the broken lower piece a moment after Cordelia landed.

He found her waiting there with three other mytre. As soon as Bruce arrived, she said, "Wait here, I'll go in first." Knowing any delay allowed for doubt she acted quickly, ducking under the broken door as she had done ages before.

Inside, the room was dark and still smelt of death. Flesh on the bone hung from hooks and she flew to rest on the chopping block in the centre of the room as she'd done before. From there she waited for her eyes to adjust to the dim light and seeing or sensing nothing to fear, she called for the others to follow.

Barry came first followed by Vall and Valora. Bruce hesitated, only for a second, before he too found his nerve and darted under the broken wooden doorway and into the musty sweet room of death.

The four mytre were already at work. Vall and Valora were busy tearing at the gladwrap that covered a tray of cut up kangaroo meat on the bench top, while Cordelia and Barry were slowly nudging the tray towards the edge of the bench. Once the children had loosened and removed some of the clear plastic cover, they joined in the task of sliding and pushing the tray of freshly cut dark red meat towards the edge of the bench. It was slow going and Cordelia thought, *There must be a lot more meat on the tray than in the past*. But gradually the tray started to slide towards its tipping point.

Bruce soon forgot his fear, as the prospect of a delicious feed overtook him. They all found their eyesight soon adjusted to the dim light in the shed, and soon Bruce could clearly see the lip of the meat tray edging towards a fall.

It fell with a clatter spilling pieces of chopped up fresh, juicy, meat across the dusty floor of the slaughter shed. Bruce leapt back as it fell and almost bolted as the metal tray clanged and rattled to the ground. But then the odour and aroma of the fresh flesh gathered in his powerful nostrils. Cordelia's promise had been fulfilled.

Bruce was in dog heaven and as Cordelia and the other mytre watched on, he went to work snatching at and eating as much of the meat as he could gather into his small jaws. In between snatched bites, Bruce said, "Delicious…" or "so nice…" or "this is amazing," But he never stopped eating long enough to say much more.

Barry, Cordelia and the chicks flew down and snatched up a little of the meat too, making sure to avoid any that Bruce had his eye on. Before too long, everyone in the shed had eaten their fill of the juicy, tender diced kangaroo meat.

Bruce could hardly move and if the deadly Yrarbil was able to return, Bruce doubted the vile creature could fit him in his mouth, so full and expanded was his belly.

Cordelia and her kin were also full, and she called for them all to select one piece of meat to carry to her other friends; the four yard-dogs. Once Bruce was outside, all four mytre left the shed through the same missing wooden gap in the door and flew across to the kennels. There they used the 'swoop, snatch, swing, spring, and sail' technique to deliver a small piece of meat to each of the resting dogs.

"It's Cordelia," one barked, as they all snatched up their small gifts.

"Thank you," the youngest dog, Martin, called, as they circled above the kennels and flew off, following Bruce back to the veranda at the norzela nest.

"I'm afraid we have to bid you farewell, friend," Cordelia said, sadly. "It's time we set off west again in search of Gary."

"Can't you stay longer?" Bruce begged. Before belching because of his full belly.

"We have to fly, old friend," Cordelia called, as she rose into the sky behind her children and Barry. "You take care, you brave and wonderful dog you."

"Thank you," they all called, with Vall adding, "it was lovely to 'meet' you."

-0-

Cordelia had never flown to the western mountains before and the four mytre flew together gathering height and dropping with a twirl as the air currents allowed. They could see they were further west than they had imagined and after the past two passages of Elppa, all the mytre were exhausted. Few mytre migrate and even fewer leave their territorial skies, so for Cordelia and her kin, this was a marathon adventure, but they flew on, aided by the gyre and zephyr of the dry hot inner plains.

The mountains were slowly growing closer, and Cordelia could see they would be there before Egnaro's arrival. She was glad, because she could also see Vall was starting to tire and would need to rest soon.

Suddenly she was aware of a massive bird at her right wing. *An eagle*, she thought with alarm. None of the mytre had seen it flying above them and none saw it glide into formation with Cordelia, until it was there on her wing.

"I'm Cord…" she was about to say, hoping her name might help appease the bird.

"I know who you are… bird," the eagle said, adding, "I am Gloria…"

Cordelia was immediately shocked. If this wasn't Gary, they were surely in great danger, and she instantly began to consider how they could all escape or if indeed any of them would manage to avoid the massive bird's talons.

"Oh, yes… I have two talons," Gloria said, although it wasn't said as a threat, or with any malice. Cordelia thought, *How did this bird know I was thinking about the number of talons she had. I know Gary has only one, but why would this bird think to mention her own talons*? Cordelia looked over at Barry and signalled for him and the young mytre to start to descend.

"Do you mean to harm us?" Cordelia asked. Adding, "And how is it that you know who I am, Gloria the…?" She paused. "What is your full title, Gloria?" Cordelia asked boldly.

"You are indeed a wise and brave mytre. My father said you would be. I am Gloria… daughter of Gary, the wedge tail eagle, only son of Garth, grandson of Graham, great grandson of George, and descendant of the Great Gus from the western mountain cliffs."

"Gary… has a daughter… that's wonderful news," Cordelia cried, genuinely amazed. Adding in the same breath, "Is he nearby… have we found him?"

"He saw you from afar. His eyesight is legendary, and he sent me to guide you to our home in the western mountain cliffs. Bring your companions and follow me to our eyrie."

Cordelia called after her descending kin and asked them to follow her as they were guided by Gloria back to Gary's eyrie home.

Barry and the two children took some convincing as they had only ever seen eagles as potential keere, but they knew this had been their mission and they agreed to follow Cordelia and Gloria to the high mountain side.

"You'll be safe and welcomed by Gary," Cordelia said, as she introduced Gloria to her family.

There was room in the nest for all four mytre. Gary was waiting for them there as they approached.

"Cordelia, Cordelia the brave," he called.

Cordelia led in the flight and flew directly at Gary taking him in a warm feathered embrace, as Barry, Vall, and Valora flew in and perched on the lip of the massive nest.

"Finally, I've come to your home, and I'm so glad to see you again, old friend," she cried. Adding, "Are you well?"

"I am very well, but getting old I can tell, as the winter breezes cut me to my very quill. Some days, here on the high cliff I can feel the wind shoot through me as if I still had those hard stones you took out still embedded in my wing and flesh. But I am well indeed and more so for the joy of your visit, but why have you come so far?"

"I wanted you to meet my family," Cordelia said, honestly, as she introduced them. "Barry is my partner, and these are Vall and Valora our two first hatchlings," Cordelia explained pointing to the respective mytre. Gary could see the fear on their faces and the nerve it was taking for them to stay perched on the nest's outer twigs.

"Pleased to meet you, your mother and you are welcome at my eyrie any time, and you will be safe and protected under my wing. No harm will come to you." He paused and bowed low to each mytre. "Your mother saved my life and helped me fly again after I'd been shot and injured..." He bowed low to Cordelia too, and said genuinely, "She is the bravest and most compassionate mytre I have ever known. Her family is very welcome here... you are all honoured guests, and I'm glad you are here."

"Stop it,' Cordelia said, blushing and feeling embarrassed by the compliments. "I didn't come for thanks and tall tales... and anyway you were the one who saved my life and the valley when you killed Lord Kratt."

"Enough," Gary said, changing the subject by saying, "I see you have met Gloria, my daughter, on the wing, and this is my partner, Glenda." As he spoke another large eagle flapped into a landing on the rock ledge next to the nest.

"My pleasure to meet you," she said as she folded her massive wings and hopped into the nest next to Gary.

Cordelia looked suddenly sheepish and whispered to Gary, "Can we talk? I have something urgent and important to ask you."

He nodded and looked surprised at the subdued nature of her question, but recognising there was something else on her mind besides introductions, he agreed to talk to her in private, on the wing.

"Forgive me, Glenda," Cordelia said, shyly adding, "We'll not be gone long." Gary took off first and was followed swiftly by Cordelia as they glided down and then flapped easily into the darkening sky as Egnaro began to rise.

-0-

"What did he say?" Barry asked of Cordelia once they had returned.

"I'll let Gary tell you with Elppa's glow," she whispered, not wishing to disturb the sleeping children, or wake Gary's kin.

Although Barry was exhausted from their long flight he could hardly rest, and he fidgeted all through Egnaro's passage. The high eyrie was windswept and cold, and while it offered a magnificent view over the western plains, it made Barry feel dizzy. Even he thought it was a strange feeling for a bird so used to flight and height. He was nervous and still wasn't sure he fully trusted the strange and massive hunters.

Clearly Cordelia had made a powerful impression on their host, but eagles had always been mytre killers, and it took all his courage, trust in Cordelia, and will, to accept that he was there in the eagle's nest, with his partner and children.

But Cordelia had impressed on him their need to visit the eagle and to test out her unusual request. He had originally agreed to go with her, but at first, he'd not agreed to taking the children, but she had known he'd give in and allow them to come. "After all," she'd argued, "who will look after them... and think of the benefits they will gain from an adventure in the wider world beyond the valley." He knew she was right, and in time, he agreed, keeping his fear and dread in check as the journey progressed. But now they were actually at the eagle's nest, now they had met the giant birds, his courage began to faulter, and doubt grew with the cold and wind.

Barry woke with a start.

"Stop it... it tickles," Vall was saying, with a giggle.

"No... not under my wing, no... no..." Valora squealed, before crying out playfully, "My turn."

Barry was at first alarmed, but he soon saw it was Gloria playing with his children on the rock ledge next to the nest. Having never met an eagle before, each mytre child had embraced the adventure and were in the middle of a two on one tickling game with the young eagle child.

"They look happy," Gary said to Barry, as he nodded toward the playful trio. Barry looked confused and was still blinking the sleep from his eyes, but he had to agree they all seemed to be getting on very well.

Cordelia was at his side, and she asked Gary, "Have you had time to consider my request?"

"We have," Gary replied. He looked disappointed and Cordelia braced for the worst. "We spoke about your idea as Egnaro passed. "I'm afraid I cannot go."

Cordelia's heart sank. Then he went on, "Glenda and I have lived in the western mountains overlooking the wide dry plains all our lives. These are the only cliffs we have known; this is the only sky we have flown, it's our only home. My trip to your valley many passings of Elppa ago was the farthest I have travelled, and I am older now and still feel the effects of my injuries." He paused again and looked directly at Cordelia. Then he looked at Barry. He shook his head slowly.

"I'm sorry, I know you'd like Glenda and I to come to your valley and watch over your kin and friends and help defend you when keere things threaten your home, and young... but we can't go."

Cordelia began to say, "I... we understand, we knew we were asking a lot and without justification, we had no right."

Gary held up a huge wing to silence her. "I said I cannot go... that we cannot go," Gary added, gesturing to Glenda. "But we spoke as a family, and Gloria and her partner Griffen would like to come with you and live on the escarpment shelf you described. They will welcome an opportunity to travel away from the hot dry interior and build a new home overlooking the valley..."

"And...' Gloria added, "we agree that no harm will come to any of the valley mytre by our beaks or talons." Griffen was nestled close into the cliff-face on the rock ledge, trying to stay out of the wind. Cordelia or Barry hadn't seen him, and they were startled when he spoke.

"I'd be happy to live in a cooler place with plenty of trees and the company of a clan of magnificent mytre...a team of escarpment eagles, and valley mytre. It sounds delightful," Griffen declared as he ruffled his wonderful plumage.

-0-

The mytre stayed two more passings of Egnaro, with the eagles showing them every kindness and courtesy. Cordelia told them about the lizard invasion and the cat, and how she had been injured and treated kindly again by some norzela.

"They are not all thugs with guns," Cordelia declared referring to the older brother norzela she and Gary had encountered at the station.

"Some seem to care and help us," Cordelia concluded.

"But many, if not hurtful or unhelpful, they are simply careless and unthinking, being more inclined to care about their own needs and making the world suitable only for norzela to occupy," Barry speculated.

-0-

Cordelia, Barry, Vall and Valora returned to the valley without the eagles. It meant they had time to call an elpitlum and explain that they had been successful in their quest to secure help with the valley security. Some of the mytre remained unsure, thinking that no eagle would ever come to the valley, and the issue would be mute. However, after a long conversation and explanation, the majority agreed that having help close at hand in case of invasion, or another cat attack, was a useful asset for the Valley Clan.

When Gloria and Griffen arrived after the next passage of Elppa, it was Vall and Valora who showed them to the eagle's new home on the escarpment and guided them around the valley and eucalypt forest.

Many of the non-mytre birds were shocked and scared as the two huge eagles flew lazily above the valley, but word soon spread that the eagles had come to protect the valley and that they were allies of the Valley Clan. It took ages for most mytre to adjust, but eventually the new allies were accepted and made welcome, so that peace truly blossomed across the valley.

18

CORDELIA'S SPIRIT

Yeah, yeah, and the wind is talkin'
Yeah, yeah, for the very first time
With a melody that pulls you towards it
Paintin' pictures of paradise

Beyoncé – (The Lion King) 'Spirit' (2019)

CORDELIA AND BARRY sat together on a branch of their home tree looking out over the western side of the valley. Their offspring had fledged and grown, matured and flown, and they'd had many other broods as the years passed. They had watched as the norzela child in the norzela nest grew too. They saw that she had gone for a long while; years, before coming back to the nest to live with her parents and raise her own young. The Valley Clan visited the norzela nest regularly and often gathered to celebrate or sing on the lawn.

Jock passed years before the daughter returned and as he had become a great friend of the clan, the mytre sang a lament for him, into whatever spiritual home dogs go to. Tran and Val had watched it all from their seats on their back veranda and remained mystified but delighted with the magpies of the valley.

Cordelia and Barry taught all their offspring the skills needed to survive, and they were all recruited into the scouting patrols and rapid response squad, although threats from keere things seemed to diminish as the Valley Clan allies and friends grew under the watchful eyes of Gloria and Griffen.

They had kept their word to never harm a Valley Clan mytre and they had built a large and beautiful eyrie on the escarpment shelf that had once been the dark raven's home. Cordelia visited them often and all her children became firm friends with the majestic and terrifying hunters.

Barry passed one summer, when the high hot wind blew in from the north. He had been teaching the 'swoop, snatch, swing, spring, and sail' technique to some new scouting patrol recruits when his heart simply gave way. He was halfway through a display when he fell from the sky and rolled and tumbled until he came to rest under a tall pine tree near the norzela park.

Cordelia was heartbroken and many of the Valley Clan believed that she never really recovered. After his passing and their collective carolling that lasted almost a full passing of Elppa, Cordelia was more often alone, flying up to the high escarpment to meet with Gloria and Griffen, or flying high above the valley watching over her home and reflecting or thinking about her long life.

She often recalled her flight and fight for the valley with Lord Kratt, the destruction of the fire and flood, the brazen advance of the lizard army and Lord Silas and the time of terror brought on by the ginger cat. The years since had been relatively peaceful, and the Valley Clan had grown in number, strength and wisdom.

The clarity of her thoughts of Bruce and the station diminished with the passing years, but if the dry flat treeless station plain came to mind, it always brought a lightness to her heart, a spark to her spirit, and a smile to her face. She also remembered her old injuries and when the weather was cold or if Egnaro sent a cool chill, her wing ached and her head hurt, and she would shiver with the thought of the dark norzela cage, the wire cage on the escarpment, and the teeth of the cat gripping her flesh.

She spent hours with her own young, or the chicks of her children. Many of whom now lived in peace and safety in the valley and these gave her the greatest joy she could have imagined.

Cordelia pecked at the soil and grass along the side of the driveway that ran up to the norzela nest on the western side of the valley. She ignored a few beetles and only tugged half-heartedly at a worm that she found near the root of a short bush. Her appetite had diminished of late, and she walked slowly along, pecking more at the stones and rocks near the side of the road than at food.

Elppa was setting and the air had turned cooler as the shadows began to grow across the valley floor.

Suddenly, she was aware of a large black and white mytre at her side. The visitor looked unnaturally large and was certainly the biggest mytre Cordelia had seen, being a half larger again than Cordelia. She would normally challenge a stranger, on the Valley Clan lands, but something about the mytre made her relax and accept their presence with a sense of calm.

"Cordelia?" the visitor asked quietly, reverently.

"Yes..." Cordelia replied.

"Are you feeling tired?" The visitor asked kindly. "You have worked so hard for the valley mytre and for your friends and family here in your lovely valley... you must be tired?"

"I am," she agreed, with a sigh, "so tired."

"Come and rest with me under the shade of the tall ghost gun that has been your home all your life."

"I would welcome a rest," Cordelia agreed. Both mytre walked or hop-stepped toward the massive roots of the gum.

"Settle here," the stranger said, pointing to a comfortable leaf bed nest between the tree roots.

"You are not from the Valley Clan, are you?" Cordelia asked softly, as she settled into the soft bed of leaves.

"No," the stranger replied, "but I am also called Cordelia, like you." Cordelia looked at the large mytre.

"I know you, don't I?" Cordelia asked.

"All mytre know me," the stranger replied in a soft, gentle voice.

"I am Cordelia the Great, the mytre from your stories and myth. I am the Cordelia who leads Elppa's Great Flock, and I have come to ask if you would like to join my flock?"

"But I'm needed here in the valley. I have my chicks, my young, my friends to look out for..." she protested.

"They'll be fine, you will always be looking over them from my flock, Cordelia the brave... the wise, the forgiving, the honest, the loving and the compassionate. Friend of Gary the wedge tail eagle, only son of Garth, grandson of Graham, great grandson of George, and descendant of the Great Gus from the western mountain cliffs and friend to his daughter Gloria and her partner Griffen."

The mythical Cordelia paused and said kindly, "You have many friends who love you. Cordelia, you will be welcome in my flock, and I would be honoured to have you among the greatest mytre under Elppa's glow." Cordelia could feel her head rest to one side as she drifted off to sleep.

"Barry and Corzell, your father, your mother, Corselia, and Kratatora, and many, many, others are waiting to sing you into the greatest clan of all. Elppa's clan of gifted, chosen and deserving mytre."

Cordelia felt a sudden strength as she lifted gently into the sky. A strength she'd never felt before. Suddenly after feeling tired and worn out for so long, she felt a power she had never felt in her wings before, as she lifted effortlessly into the air, rising higher... above the great gum, that had been her nest tree and home... above the valley and above the escarpment, above... the world where she felt the clarity and beauty of Elppa's warmth, light and love. *Beautiful*, she thought.

ACKNOWLEDGEMENTS

No written work of any merit gets published without the support of a great publisher. As such, I must acknowledge Morris Publishing Australia, and in particular, Elaine Ouston, who has supported and advised the development of the books in the Cordelia series. Her clear and level-headed advice and guidance have been excellent and very much appreciated.

Cordelia's Spirit is about a place that is home to several clans of magpie (called mytre in the story). The main character is a female mytre called Cordelia who is born into a conflict for clan dominance and who needs to navigate the challenges and threats of mytre life, and who grows to help lead and guide her new Valley Clan to safety and peace.

No work of fiction comes completely from the author's mind. This story is no different, and it grew from reading similar books about the world from an animal's perspective. Most notable amongst them was Richard Adams '*Watership Down*' (1972).

However, the real inspiration for a magpie focused story came from my love of the Australian bush and my encounters with the harsh realities of living in rural Australia. Therefore, I have also tried to capture something of the magic of the Australian outback and Australia wildlife in *The Valley*. Mostly though, the unique behaviour, songs and habits of the many magpies that visit my garden each day inspired me. This book is for them.

As I watched magpies feed and sing, I started to wonder if magpies might have a story of their own to tell. I knew Cordelia did. Watching them I started to view magpies in a different way. As a result, I read Gisela Kaplan's wonderful book, '*Australian Magpie: biology and behaviour of an unusual songbird*' (2nd Ed) (2022). This gave me all sorts of insights that I was able to lend to *The Valley* mytre and I hope I have done justice to magpies in the same way she has with her book.

I have borrowed Cordelia's name from a character in William Shakespeare's play 'King Lear.' Lear's daughter, Cordelia, is too honest and is subsequently banished from his kingdom because she will not overplay her love for her father, the King. Really though, I just liked the name Cordelia and Shakespeare's character lent her name to the lead character in this book.

I also consulted a number of other written sources in developing *The Valley* and Cordelia's character. These include:

John W. Wrigley and Murray Fagg's book *'Australian Native Plants; cultivation, use in landscaping and propagation.* (Concise Edition) (2023).

Louise Egerton's *'Know your Birds; Australia's Most Common Birds'* (Revised Edition) (2019)

Matthew Jones and Duade Paton's book, *'Australian birds in pictures'* (2021).

Jeff Davies, Peter Menkhorst, Danny Rogers, Rohan Clarke, Peter Marsack, and Kim Franklin's little book, *'The Compact Australian Bird Guide'* (2022).

Peter Stanley's insightful and heartrending book; *'Black Saturday at Steels*

Creek', (2013) the story of the Black Saturday bushfires that killed in total, 173 people in February 2009.

Other aspects of *Cordelia's Spirit* were inspired by reading about the challenges feral cats pose to Australia's native wildlife, and the issues faced by Glossy Black Cockatoos, as they struggle with land clearance and the destruction brought about by bush fires. I hope the story relays a strong message about caring for the fauna and flora of the Australian bush and our natural habitat.

As well, I am glad of the proofreading skills of a number of friends who diligently read through the text and made comments or offered advice at several points in the story.

A POEM: THE MAGPIE'S CALL

In their black suits they came mourning, to the grave site near the gum.

Silence gripped the group there forming, as they gathered – looking glum.

Her two boys stood near their mother, as she bowed her head in grief.

Guttural sobs she tried to smother; nothing now gave her relief.

Long grey clouds had killed the dawning, and it left them feeling numb,

as they waited, 'neth an awning, for the hearse to slowly come.

A shard of crimson anguish stung and stabbed her heart with pain,

her husband taken far too young; now her tears fell like spring rain.

Her friends had gathered at her side, sharing tragedy and loss.

In solidarity they cried, "We will help you bear your cross."

"Your husband loved the land," they said. Calling, "To it he'll return."

It left her feeling cold and dread, and it made her stomach churn.

There was nothing they could do or say to vanquish her despair.

Her torment wouldn't go away; heartache bloomed beyond compare.

She held her boys close to her hip, as the casket dropped from view.

Descending - down and down it sank – as her heart was torn in two.

Above a calling magpie sang; softly carolling his death.

It's rippled call from gum tree rang; joyous singing – took her breath.

No prayers or pious church choir song; sang her husband to the ground.

A magpie's gurgle came along, and her sorrow turned around.

There was something in its calling, that released her dampened hope.

Like her husband's spirit falling, to embraced her so she'd cope.

It was then the magpie's singing, kissed her like the glow of dawn.

With her husband's spirit winging, now her hope could be reborn.

Soon the funeral passed from memory, she moved on but always knew.

Like the rubbing power of emery, or the glistening shine of dew.

There was something of her lost love, in the magpie's gurgling throat.

A feathered angel from above, offering comfort with each note.

COMMENTS ABOUT VARIOUS ASPECTS OF THE STORY

Some comments about the Glossy Black Cockatoos:

Glossy black cockatoos feature in the story of *Cordelia's Heart*. Their scientific name is *Calyptorhynchus lathami (in the story you can see what motivated their names: the male is called Cal, and the female is called Lathami).* The information provided about them is accurate, for they are indeed dangerously close to becoming extinct. Only small populations remain on Kangaroo Island, in South Australia, some in south-eastern Queensland, eastern Victoria, and parts of eastern New South Wales. They are the smallest of the black cockatoo family, and they feed almost exclusively on the cone seed pods of the She-oak tree or casuarina tree.

They will eat eucalyptus, angophoras, acacia, and hakea tree seeds but their favourite food is casuarina seed. This is one of the reasons they are struggling to survive, as She-oak habitats and forests dwindle across many parts of their normal range, mostly because of land clearing or bushfires. As a result, they are a protected species in New South Wales.

Male and female glossy blacks are dimorphic with males having a black-brown body, brown-black head and a red or red and orange-yellow tail. Females, however, have yellow patches on their heads and tails, which may also be slightly redder. They only have one egg every one or two years, with the male bringing the female food while she sits on the egg for about thirty days.

The nests are always close to their food source (She-oaks) and they build nests in the hollows of dead or living eucalyptus trees.

They are monogamous and like the company of just one or two other birds and are rarely seen in larger groups. But they do gather in larger groups when they are mating or gathering around a watering hole. They are not as noisy as other cockatoos making a soft or gentle '*tarr-ed*' sound. Finally, the glossy black will almost always feed by standing on its right leg and feeding exclusively from their left claw and foot. Glossy blacks are not shy of humans, so they can be approached even when they are eating, and they may not fly away immediately. More information about them can be found here:

http://wwf.org.au.blogs/7-amazing -facts-about-the-glossy-black-cockatoo/

http://backyardbuddies.org.au/backyard-buddies/glossy-blacl-cockatoo/

-0-

Some comments about the nocturnal calls of the male Willie Wagtail:

In a study by Ashton Dickerson, Therésa Jones and Michelle Hall, from the University of Melbourne, they speculated that there was evidence to support the anecdotal reports that male willie-wagtails do indeed sing at the full moon. Over the three years of their study, they recorded and observed the songs of willie-wagtails across the state of Victoria, confirming that male willie-wagtails, observed over eight complete lunar cycles, in four rural locations across Victoria, did indeed sing in line with the brightness of the moon – essentially making sure they are both seen and heard. Willie-wagtails, it seems, are indeed the werewolf of the bird world.

They also observed that they have a 'twinkling' song, often described as sounding like they are saying, '*sweet pretty creature*'. They are also known as the 'shepherd's companion', as they are commonly seen around livestock, feeding on the insects attracted to the herds. Significantly, their study showed that nocturnal songs are from chorusing males during the breeding season exclusively and that nocturnal song rates increase with lunar illumination.

Their work provides a foundation for hypothesizing the function of nocturnal song and contributes to understanding these patterns on a global level.

Their publication is: Dickerson, A, Jones, T and Hall, M. (2020). The effect of Variation in Moonlight on Nocturnal song of a Diurnal Bird Species. Journal of <u>Behavioural Ecology and Sociobiology</u>*. Vol 74 No. 109.*

-0-

Some comments about Feral Cats in Australia:

Cats make great pets, however, when they are abandoned or become feral, they can be exposed to dangers themselves (such as contagious diseases, speeding cars, poisons, and attacks by dogs and cruel humans) or, and this is more common, they can themselves be very dangerous to native animals. It is estimated that feral cats kill approximately, 75 million native animals every night across Australia, including birds, frogs, small mammals, and reptiles.

Feral cats are the direct result of the irresponsible actions of people who abandon their unsterilised cats or allow them to roam outdoors unsupervised. One study in Victoria revealed that 13 per cent of cats had a litter prior to being desexed. Sadly, lots of kittens don't find loving homes and many are either surrendered to shelters, and eventually euthanised or they are set free and abandoned, to fend for themselves, sometimes becoming feral.

It is not just feral cats that are deadly for Australian native wildlife though. Domestic cats that are able to roam around urban and rural areas retain their hunting instincts, no matter how well fed they are. Most cat guardians are in denial about the number of animals their cats kill. One study found that they see only about 23 per cent of their cat's victims. If allowed outdoors, all cats will terrorise, maim, and kill native birds and other small wild animals, which are not equipped to deal with non-native predators. These animals die from puncture wounds and from being crushed by cat's jaws.

In 2015, the Australian government announced that it intended to cull more than 2 million feral cats by 2020 through shooting, trapping, and poisoning. However, feral cats are wary of humans and trapping may be the only effective way to catch and if necessary, euthanise them. This may then take them out of the environment humanely. As a preventive measure, more states need to introduce laws requiring cat guardians to have their animals desexed – as South Australia and Western Australia have already done – and to keep their cats indoors, as is already mandatory in areas of Canberra and Melbourne.

What can you do? There are many ways people can help protect Australian wildlife from feral cats, including the following:

Never leave your cat outdoors unattended.

Always adopt – never buy an animal from a breeder or pet shop. Hundreds of thousands of healthy cats are euthanised at animal shelters every year, simply because there aren't enough good homes for them. By adopting from a rescue centre or shelter, you'll save a life and avoid lining the pockets of businesses or individuals who are contributing to the overpopulation problem.

Have your cats desexed.

More information can be sourced here:

https://www.peta.org.au/issues/wildlife/feral-cats/

-0-

Some comments on Bowerbirds:

The Bowerbird family has 27 species in eight subsets. Their diet consists mainly of fruit but may also include insects (especially for nestlings), flowers, nectar and in some species, leaves. The satin and spotted bowerbirds are sometimes considered agricultural pest due to their habit of feeding on introduced fruit and vegetable crops and have occasionally been killed by affected orchardists.

The bowerbirds are mainly located in Australia and Papua New Guinea, with ten species endemic to New Guinea, eight endemic to Australia, and two found in both. Although their distribution is cantered on the tropical regions of New Guinea and northern Australia, some species extend into central, western, and southeastern Australia. They occupy a range of different habitats, including rainforest, eucalyptus, and acacia forest, and shrublands. While the females are unequivocally drab, in some species the males have bright golden-yellow and sometimes black markings.

One group with particularly inconspicuous plumage in males as well as females, but loud meowing calls, is known as 'catbirds' although not all of these are related to bowerbirds and some live in the Americas and Africa. As well the catbirds are monogamous, with males raising chicks with their partners, but all other bowerbirds are polygynous, with females building the nest and raising the young alone.

These latter species are commonly dimorphic, with the female being drabber in colour. Female bowerbirds build a nest by laying soft materials, such as leaves, ferns, and vine tendrils, on top of a loose foundation of sticks, the bower is not a nest.

All Papuan bowerbirds lay one egg, while Australian species lay one to three with laying intervals of two days. Eggs hatch after 19 to 24 days, depending on the species.

Bowerbirds as a group have the longest life expectancy of any of their family with the green catbird and satin bowerbird, having life expectancies of around eight to ten years and one satin bowerbird has been known to live for twenty-six years. For comparison, the common raven has not been known to live longer than 21 years.

The most notable characteristic of bowerbirds is their complex and extraordinarily courtship and mating behaviour. To initiate the mating ritual, males build a bower to attract mates. There are two types of bowers; one constructed by placing sticks around a sapling with the bower having a hut-like roof. The other type builds bowers as an avenue-type bower, made of two walls of vertically placed sticks, as the satin bowerbird does.

Although some species of catbirds do not construct either bowers or display courts. In and around the bower, the male places a variety of brightly coloured objects he has collected. These objects — usually different among each species — may include hundreds of shells, leaves, flowers, feathers, stones, berries, and even discarded plastic items, coins, nails, rifle shells, or pieces of glass.

The males spend hours arranging this collection. Bowers within a species share a general form but do show significant variation, and the collection of objects reflects the biases of males of each species and its ability to procure items from the habitat, often stealing them from neighbouring bowers.

Several studies of different species have shown that colours of decorations males use on their bowers match the preferences of females. In addition to the bower construction and ornamentation, male birds perform involved courtship displays to attract the female. Research suggests the male adjusts his performance based on success and female response.

Mate-searching females commonly visit multiple bowers. Often returning to preferred bowers several times and watching the male's elaborate courtship displays and inspecting the quality of the bower. Through this process the female reduces the set of potential mates. Many females end up selecting the same male, and many under-performing males are left without copulations. Females mated with top-mating males tend to return to the male the next year and search less.

Young females tend to be more easily threatened by intense male courtship, and these females tend to choose males based on traits not dependent on male courtship intensity. The high degree of effort directed at mate choice by females and the large skews in mating success directed at males with quality displays suggests that sexual ornaments are indicators of general health and heritable disease resistance.

This complex mating behaviour, with its highly valued types and colours of decorations, has led some researchers to regard the bowerbirds as among the most behaviourally complex species of bird. It also provides some of the most compelling evidence that the extended phenotype of a species can play a role in sexual selection and indeed act as a powerful mechanism to shape its evolution. As seems to be the case for humans. Inspired by their seemingly extreme courtship rituals, Charles Darwin discussed both bowerbirds and birds of paradise in his writings.

In addition, many species of bowerbird are superb vocal mimics, copying for example, pigs, waterfalls, and human chatter. Satin bowerbirds commonly mimic other local species as part of their courtship display. Bowerbirds have also been observed creating optical illusions in their bowers to appeal to mates. They arrange objects in the bower's court area from smallest to largest, creating a forced perspective which holds the attention of the female for longer. Males with objects arranged in a way that have a strong optical illusion are likely to have higher mating success.

Source: https://en.wikipedia.org/wiki/Bowerbird